A Visit to Russia In the Autumn of 1862

SALZWASSER
VERLAG

Henry Moor

A Visit to Russia In the Autumn of 1862

Reprint of the original, first published in 1863.

1st Edition 2022 | ISBN: 978-3-37500-774-4

Verlag (Publisher): Salzwasser Verlag GmbH, Zeilweg 44, 60439 Frankfurt, Deutschland
Vertretungsberechtigt (Authorized to represent): E. Roepke, Zeilweg 44, 60439 Frankfurt, Deutschland
Druck (Print): Books on Demand GmbH, In de Tarpen 42, 22848 Norderstedt, Deutschland

A VISIT TO RUSSIA

IN THE AUTUMN OF 1862.

BY

HENRY MOOR, Esq.

With Illustrations.

LONDON:

1863.

PREFACE.

Since this record of a hasty tour in Russia was sent to *Bentley's Miscellany*, three subjects alluded to in it have received their denouément.

The ordinance of February, 1861, has come into full effect, the serfs are free, and in many parts of the country have celebrated their emancipation by *Te Deums* in their cathedrals and churches.

The second event is the insurrection in Poland, which has assumed very formidable dimensions. What the result may be it is difficult to foretel, but, according to French statements, it is not impossible that Russian Poland may, with the acquiescence of the Emperor Alexander, be constituted an independent kingdom, with the Grand-Duke Constantine for its sovereign.

The third is, that the new system for regulating the manufacture and sale of spirituous liquors has become the law of the land—an event which in too many localities has been celebrated by the humbler classes in a manner savouring of anything but total abstinence. When the first brush of the excitement has passed away, it is to be hoped that they will sober down to a more rational state of enjoyment.

CONTENTS.

CHAPTER VI.

CHAPTER VII.

CHAPTER VIII.

CHAPTER IX.

CHAPTER X.

CHAPTER XI.

A VISIT

TO

RUSSIA IN THE AUTUMN OF 1862.

CHAPTER I.

TO BERLIN—RUSSIAN FRONTIER—PASSPORTS —WILNA—PSKOFF.

HAVING received an invitation from a Russian friend and his lady to pay them a visit in the autumn of this year at their country-house in Russia, and being somewhat tired of the ordinary routes, I determined to accept it, and go in search of "fresh fields and pastures new." So, having obtained a promise from my wife that her luggage should be of the smallest possible dimensions, we soon found ourselves at Cologne the unsavoury.

Having missed the next morning's express train to Berlin, we took the mid-day one to Minden, a fortified and very pretty town on this side of Hanover. Here, of course, we looked for that "wood-crowned height" on which Eliza is poetically stated to have stood, and been "o'er Minden's plain spectatress of the fight." As, however, there were more "wood-crowned heights" than one, and as no one recollected anything about the lady, we took our choice of one of them, consoling ourselves with the sage reflection, that if it were not that one, it must be another.

On the following afternoon we took the train to Berlin, arriving there at ten o'clock at night, and a pretty scene of confusion there was in finding one's luggage. It really was the worst managed thing of the kind we had ever seen. However, after some time and much labour we "came by our own," and reached the Hotel Royal, the master of which was uncommonly polite, until I told him that we only intended remaining there until the following night, upon which he immediately vanished, leaving us to the tender mercies of a very independent waiter. On our return through Berlin we did not put his politeness to a second test.

We passed the next day seeing all that was to be seen in Berlin, and in providing ourselves with Russian money. We found the Unter den Linden somewhat shorn of its pristine glory, the trees presenting a very sickly, and in one, though not in the best sense, *shady*, appearance, caused, we were told, by the gas-pipes among their roots, and the gas-lamps among their leaves. We quitted Berlin by the express train at night, intending to make a halt at Wilna, to which place our friends were to send a Russ-and-French-speaking courier to meet us. After twenty hours' travelling in a most comfortable carriage, in which we found water laid on for our morning ablutions, we arrived at Wierzbolow, the Russian frontier, where the formalities of examining passports and baggage took place. The passport business did not occupy much time, and before leaving the frontier ours was handed back to us, rather to my surprise, for I had read that foreigners' passports were detained until they were leaving the country. A stamp was, however, affixed, showing the day on which we had passed into the Russian territory, and which stamp was to be used against us afterwards, as we found to our cost.

The examination of the baggage was not so easily got through, as we unfortunately arrived at a time when a large number of Russian families were returning to their homes, and, as usual, carrying about twenty times the quantity of baggage which a well-regulated English family would think necessary. The result of this was a considerable delay, and much pushing, crowding, and nervous anxiety on the part of certain middle-aged, sharp-looking females, whom I put down in my own mind as *marchandes de modes* doing the revenue. Here we had to take fresh tickets, and get our luggage registered for Wilna. How we should have got on amongst the porters and subordinates, without the kind assistance of two Russian gentlemen, whose acquaintance we had made on the road, it is difficult to say. Thanks to them, however, our path was made pretty smooth. One of these gentlemen—who was a large landed proprietor not far from Moscow—gave us a hearty invitation to go and see him at his country-house, and have a week's wolf-hunting. The other was returning from the London Exhibition, and said that he had received so much hospitality in England, that it was a pleasure to him to be of use in his own country to English people. It may be said here, once for all, that the hospitality which we received, and which was offered to us, during our stay in Russia, made a great impression on us. We had heard that, since the Crimean war, English people were at a discount in Russian estimation, and were consequently all the more delighted with our kindly reception at the hands of all with whom we came in contact.

We arrived at Wilna at three o'clock in the morning, and were much relieved by finding the courier waiting for us on the platform. We had made the discovery at the frontier that it is not pleasant to be in a country whose language is a sealed book to the stranger, and we did not contemplate with pleasure the arrival at three o'clock in the morning in a strange place, not knowing where to go, nor how to express our wishes. The country from Berlin to Wilna presents nothing worth seeing, and, indeed, the same may be said of the country to Petersburg, Moscow, and Nijni Novgorod. The traveller passes over a level country, and does not meet with even the ghost of a tunnel. At the station at Wilna we found a regular London brougham with a pair of horses waiting for us, and in about a quarter of an hour afterwards arrived at an hotel called the Niszkouski. What that means I could not find out. Here we had tolerably clean rooms, and high charges.

Wilna is a half-Polish, half-Russian town, with a population of about sixty thousand inhabitants, nearly one-half of whom are Jews. Wilna was conquered and taken by the Russians in 1794. It was formerly the capital of Lithuania, and is situated at the conflux of the navigable river Wilia and the Wileyka. The streets are very narrow and badly laid out. On the Castle Hill stand the ruins of a palace of the Jagellons, formerly Grand-Dukes of Lithuania, one of whom married Hedvige, then Queen of Poland, by which Lithuania and Poland became united. This event took place about the end of the fourteenth century, but it does not appear that any legislative union was formed until the Diet of Lubin in 1569. There is here a very ancient cathedral, with numerous churches, one of which is particularly curious, being built of dark-coloured bricks with very white mortar lines, causing in the deepset doorway and window-tracings a singular and novel appearance. The cathedral dedicated to St. Stanislaus, and built in 1367, is well worth a visit, and amongst other curiosities contains a large number of stone statues of the saints and others, the eyes of which, being deeply carved, give an almost lifelike, though not pleasant effect. These statues are said to be many hundred years old. The university, which was founded by the Jesuits in 1580 as a college for their order, was suppressed by the Russian Government in 1832, and its library transferred to St. Petersburg.

The costumes of the droschky-drivers, or cabmen as we should call them, with their long uncombed beards, loose gowns, many-coloured sashes, and queer little hats, to say nothing of their carriages and quaint harness, are very striking to a person who sees them for the first time. Most of the ladies whom we saw were dressed in mourning, which, upon inquiry, we were told was in sympathy with the late abortive attempts at Warsaw. As they are very good looking, with elegant figures, and appeared to great advantage in black, it is to be hoped that the Government will allow them to wear it undisturbed. Indeed, the looker-on may well doubt whether a little personal coquetry is not mixed up with their national sympathy. There are some few manufactures carried on, and the trade of the place is comparatively large.

At three o'clock on the following morning we left Wilna, and arrived in the afternoon at Pskoff, the chief town of the province of that name, where our friend was waiting for us, and with him we went to the governor's house. That gentleman was on a tour through his province on duties connected principally with the serf's or peasant's question, at present causing so much discussion and difference of opinion in Russia.

Notwithstanding the governor's absence, we were most hospitably entertained, and here, for the first time, we made personal acquaintance with a Russian custom of which we had previously heard. On dinner being announced we proceeded to the dining-room, but, before taking our seats, the gentlemen proceeded to a side-table, on which was placed caviar, cheese, sardines, &c., with small slices of bread, and three or four decanters holding brandy, rum, and white liquor which they call gin, but which is not like our liquor of that name. It is, however, very good, with a strong taste of caraway-seeds. Of these viands and spirits, which pass under the name of *the zakouski*, the gentlemen are expected to partake, and though I certainly never before *began* dinner with cheese and brandy, I felt bound to do as the others did, and truth compels me to declare that I did not find my appetite any the worse for it. In fact, there is no saying, until he has tried, what a man can, or cannot, do in this world.

The town of Pskoff has sixteen thousand inhabitants, and two hotels, which are said to be good. It is the see of an archbishop, and the residence of the military governor. The manufactures consist principally of leather, sail-cloth, glass, and linen, but it is said that, unlike the rest of their countrymen, they have not much inclination for mechanics, or any kind of handicraft. The cathedral is as ancient as any in Russia, and the screen, reaching nearly to the roof, is very curious, and at the same time costly. There is a tolerably handsome building used as a club for the nobility, and a convent, or, as we should say, a nunnery. We were only admitted into the large quadrangle and thence conducted to the chapel, which is full of very old pictures and relics. On leaving, I gave the sister who conducted us some copecks, in return for which she kissed hands. The river Velikaia, running from south to north, bisects the town, which many years ago had a population of nearly eighty thousand inhabitants. Like its not distant neighbour, Novgorod Welike, its trade was diverted into a new channel by the foundation of St. Petersburg. Before that event the trade and commerce of Novgorod and Moscow used to go through Pskoff to England, France, and Germany; now they go to St. Petersburg, and thence by sea. The trade of Pskoff consists mainly of flax and fish from the great Peipus lake, the former of which finds its way to England, and the latter, when cured and dried, to the surrounding localities. Pskoff is situated on the eastern frontier of Livonia and near the northern frontier of Poland, and is stated to have been founded in the tenth century by the Grand-Duchess Olga, who was, I believe, the first Russian Princess that embraced Christianity. The province of Pskoff was formerly a republic in connexion with the Hanseatic towns, but was incorporated into the Moscow principality in 1510, after the conquest of the Novgorod republic by Ivan III. In the fifteenth century Bartory, a Hungarian, then King of the Poles, attacked the town of Pskoff, and, having effected a breach in the walls, which is shown to this day, advanced some way into the town, when the inhabitants repulsed and drove him back. Round the town the ruins of the old walls are still standing, as are also the remains of the fortifications which Peter the Great erected after the battle of Narva, in which Charles XII. of Sweden defeated the Russians.

CHAPTER II.

POSTING—PEASANTS' FÊTE—TEA-DRINKING—RUSSIAN COUNTRY-HOUSE—RUSSIAN VILLAGES AND VILLAGERS.

AFTER resting a short time at Pskoff, we started with our friend to his father's country-seat and estate, a distance of about eighty English miles. This journey we performed sometimes with four, sometimes with six horses. The charge for post-horses in Russia is not very high, four horses and the driver costing eightpence a mile. This is exclusive of the *padaroshna*, or order to the postmaster, which cost me, including the stamped paper, seven shillings. It is needless to say, that without this padaroshna the traveller gets no horses. Unless there are more than four horses, the postboy, or *yamstchik*, drives from the box; in the case of six or eight horses there is an additional yamstchik, who rides one of the leaders. These men seem to have no idea of any pace between a walk and a right down gallop. A table showing the distances between the stations, and the charge for each horse, is hung up at the post-houses, but as it is printed in the Russian language and characters, I gave it up as an impossible job. The postmaster is by law compelled to give as many horses as are ordered in the padaroshna, but he may oblige travellers to have more if the roads are very bad. Sometimes he is disposed to tell you that there are no horses at home, but a judgmatical application of warm roubles cures his temporary indisposition. The cost of posting being so cheap is owing, we were told, to the fact that the Government pays a certain annual sum to the postmasters towards the expense of maintaining horses; so that the wealthy classes, who, of course, are the only ones that use this mode of conveyance, get their travelling expenses more than half paid by the country. This anomaly, like many others, has, it is said, attracted the notice of the present Emperor, who seems bent on destroying all abuses, great or small. The Government also provides the post-houses, some of which are very good, in which travellers may dispose of their provisions, and sleep during their journeys, without paying anything. For the first four hours the road, being the high road to St. Petersburg, was excellent, though, in consequence of the railroad being open, not so much used as formerly. At the post-house, or station, as it is called, of Katergna we left the high road, and proceeded across country roads, which for four hours were very deep in sand, compelling us to have six horses. The shaking and bumping on these roads was something to recollect. At the post-house at Katergna the rooms were very clean and commodious.

A story is told of the late Emperor Nicholas, whose carriage broke down near this place about ten years ago. Although his Majesty could have taken any one of the numerous carriages of his suite, he preferred remaining here until one could be sent from St. Petersburg. To quicken the movements of his coachmaker, *et pour encourager les autres*, he telegraphed to St.

Petersburg to arrest and imprison the coach-maker who had supplied him with the unlucky one until another carriage arrived at Katergna, which, it is needless to say, made its appearance in a very short space of time.

At about nine o'clock in the evening we arrived at our destination, and on entering one of the villages at a short distance from the house, found the peasants keeping their annual fête. They were all very glad to see my friend, who received no end of invitations, in which we were included, to go to their houses and take tea, or something stronger, in which latter article some of them appeared to have already indulged. I was quite surprised to see such a crowd of apparently well-to-do, good-humoured looking, contented people, and to learn that they were the actual serfs of whom I had heard such a different description. My friend seemed to be a great favourite among them, and certainly, if working very hard in their interests constituted a claim on their gratitude, he had earned it. He is one of the committee of eight, elected and nominated, for bringing the abolition-of-serfdom-ordinance into effect in his province. Possessing a thorough English solidity of character, combined with truly liberal feelings, much ability, and a genuine desire to raise the position and secure the independence of the peasantry, he has been of invaluable service to them, and in his own neighbourhood they appear to know and appreciate it. As we were all more or less tired after the day's jolting over the sand-hills, and as our friend's wife was waiting to receive us, we declined all the invitations to tea, as well as another to drag us in our carriage through a small river, and proceeded on our way, arriving at dusk at a floating-bridge, on which we were carried to the other side of the river, and soon found ourselves comfortably seated at the tea-table, presided over by our spirituelle and hospitable hostess.

Here, for the first time, we made acquaintance with the somervar, a sort of tea-urn, but exclusively a Russian speciality, and enjoyed the Russian tea as it is drank in that country. The Russians attribute the superiority of their tea to the fact that it is sent overland from China, and does not get spoiled by the sea air. I should be inclined to think that the real reason is that it comes from provinces in China near the Russian frontier, where there is a better growth of it than in the provinces from which comes the article we use. I think, also, that they understand infusing the tea better than we do. They drink it as soon as the boiling water is poured on it, whilst we allow it to stand until it becomes as black as one's hat and as bitter as hops. The gentlemen mostly drink their tea in tumblers, without milk, sometimes adding a slice of lemon, whilst the ladies take it in cups, with any amount of cream. We were afterwards, especially when travelling on the Moscow and Nijni railroads, surprised at the large and constant use of this beverage at all hours of the day and night, but we very soon became as large consumers of it as the most native Russians themselves. Indeed, after a night in the railway carriage, we found that tumbler of tea in the early morning more exhilarating than the "blest sherbet," and more refreshing than even hock and soda-water. When at Petersburg we bought a small quantity of a fine sample of caravan tea, for which we paid at the rate of thirty-eight shillings the pound, but, of course, this was one of the fancy sorts, and not that which is in common use, which costs about six shillings and sixpence the pound. At the shop where we bought this tea, we were informed that they had some as high as seventy shillings the pound. As we were accompanied by a resident in the city who always dealt there, we knew that we were not being victimised. I mention this circumstance, as otherwise the generality of English people, who are not accustomed to hear of such charges for tea, might imagine that the St. Petersburg tea-dealer had taken advantage of the English foreigners.

Our friend's country-house was a large square building, with spacious rooms, library, and billiard-room. A long, deep verandah ran nearly the whole length of the back part of the house, looking over a pleasure-garden and the river close by. This verandah was fitted up with curtains, cushions, and tables, at which we used to breakfast, and take our fruit, coffee, and cigars after dinner. The establishment was just such a one as is met with in the country in England, where the owner is wealthy, except that the outbuildings and dependencies were larger and more numerous.

About twenty yards from the mansion was a smaller house, in which four rooms were set apart for our use, with two female and one male dvorovi, or slaves, to attend to our wants.

There was a separate building for the baths, whilst moored in the middle of the river was a bathing-house for summer use.

Then there were two large buildings for the dvorovi, numbering about forty, exclusive of children, capital stables, and so on.

The kitchen-garden was laid out like an English one, and filled with peas, cucumbers, and other vegetables, whilst the peaches and grapes from the hothouses were as rich and fine as any in England or France.

Being desirous of seeing as much as possible of the Russian peasants' mode of life and means of living, I asked my friend to accompany me to another village on his estate. I should mention that he has sixteen villages, with a population of about two thousand four hundred, the estate itself comprising about twenty-two thousand English acres. The houses of the peasants are all constructed of wood, and their great enemy is fire. To guard against its ravages, in some of the villages I saw painted on the houses, here a bucket, there a ladder, then an axe, and so on—those being the different implements which the occupiers are bound to have ready, and to bring with them on the alarm of fire being given. As education is rather a scarce commodity among the working classes, these symbols are used as a substitute for writing, which would be useless. In the cities and towns there are high towers, upon which men are stationed day and night to watch, and, when a fire occurs, to give the alarm. In the villages, however, there do not appear to be these fire-watchmen. The houses in the village which we first visited were built of wood, but of two stories, which is not usual. The owner of one that we entered pointed out a place over the oven which they use in very cold weather to sleep upon.

In nearly every room was a small picture

of the Virgin or Saviour, or some favourite saint; but in the chief room there was a larger one, with a silver lamp hanging before it. On entering the room where this latter picture is kept, it is necessary to take off your hat and remain uncovered as long as you are there. These pictures are very badly painted, but, to compensate for this deficiency, they are ornamented with little bits of silver, glass beads, imitation pearls, &c. The peasants are superstitious, and great sticklers for outward forms. From all I could learn, the priests either do not, or cannot, much enlighten them. There are a great many sects in Russia, but as long as the worship and observances of any peculiar form of religion are not plainly opposed to the laws of God or man, they are tolerated by the Government. There are one or two sects, however, which it is as well not

Vincent Brooks, lith.

RUSSIAN CHAPEL.

to describe, which are not tolerated or permitted. It is said that the lower orders fast for nearly six out of the twelve months, and work only about the same time. There are constantly recurring fast or fête days; and on these occasions they eschew meat and work, but do a good deal in the way of imbibing.

As it would be next to impossible to have a church in each village, there is generally one in some neighbouring town, or large village, to which the peasants occasionally resort; but in each village, however small, there is usually a chapel. This building contains a picture of the Saviour or Virgin, and is opened only once a year by the priest, the day on which he does so being a fixed one, and kept as the annual fête-day of the village. The people are not allowed to go into the building, but stand outside worshipping.

The men rarely pass it without taking off their hats and crossing themselves.

From the above village we walked to one not very far off, owned by the Government. Here, as in most of the Government villages, the peasantry are not so well off as those in the proprietors' villages. I am unable to account for this, especially as the Government do not claim from its tenants any unpaid labour service. In the one we visited the peasantry alleged that they had been a few years previously robbed by some of the officers appointed to manage the estate and collect the rents. It would appear that there had been a failure of crops, and the officers apprehended, or said they did, which is perhaps nearer the mark, that the peasants would not have sufficient seed-corn for the next year, so they insisted that the peasants should buy what they considered sufficient for the purpose. In vain the peasants represented that they had enough, and that if they had not, it was impossible for them, at that season of the year, to fetch it from the Government granaries in time to sow it. They were obliged to fetch it, and although, as they had foreseen, they were unable to use, were made to pay for it. But the worst of the matter was, that the poor people, being afraid to ask for a receipt, were called upon to pay for this seed-corn more than twice. At last the officer was called to account, but not until the people were nearly pauperised, the officer, strange to say, escaping unpunished. Had he been made to run the gauntlet through the village he had plundered, he would have been "the right man in the right place." But, in Russia, venality appears to be too lightly regarded.

CHAPTER III.

SERFS AND SLAVES—THE ORDINANCE OF FEBRUARY, 1861—ITS EFFECTS AND PROBABLE RESULTS.

HAVING read a great deal about the serf question in England, and hearing it constantly mentioned and discussed where I was, I determined, if possible, to master the subject, so I engaged my friend to give me as brief a statement of the matter as he could. When I went to my room at night I committed it to writing, and on the next morning read it over to him, making the alterations which he pointed out as necessary. I therefore give the following narration on the authority of one who well understands the subject, but who, I am bound and glad to state, is a warm supporter of the liberation doctrine, and may, therefore, take too sanguine a view of eventualities.

As I have previously said, this gentleman is one of the committee of eight, whose duty it is to arrange differences between the proprietors and the peasantry under the new law. He is one of the two whom the Government appoints on each committee, and belongs to the class of nobles or proprietors.

Many centuries ago, it would seem that the peasant had the use of a certain portion of land, paying, not for the land, but for his house. This payment was not made in money, but in produce, and by rendering military service in time of war. The jurisdiction over the peasant, and the gathering of these payments, or taxes, as they were then called, was granted by the sovereign to his favourites and retainers, upon the sole condition that in time of war they should appear with a certain number of armed followers, whom they were to maintain, equip, and support at their own expense. In the commencement of this system this privilege was granted for life only, but it subsequently became hereditary. Not, however, by any actual motion or consent of the Crown, but by the encroachments of the holders of the privilege.

Up to and in the middle of the sixteenth century such was the state of matters, the nobles holding the largest number of peasants, the monasteries possessing a smaller number, and the sovereign a still smaller number.

It must be borne in mind that both by the peasant and by the proprietor, whether noble or monastic, it was understood that no title to the soil of the land vested in the latter, but that all he possessed or could legally claim was the jurisdiction over the peasant, and the right to receive the taxes and enforce the military service.

The country being at that period very sparsely populated, and the land much more than sufficient for all, the peasant took and cultivated as much of it as he chose, neither the quantity nor quality being taken into account in assessing the taxes to be paid in respect of it. In fact, the peasant was taxed in respect of his house only, or, in the language of that day, in respect of his *smoke*.

At the period of which I am writing there was no census, the quantity of the land in each district was unknown, and had no ascertained boundaries, and no laws existed by which the proprietor or landed property were regulated or controlled. By degrees, however, the land began to be valuable, being better cultivated, and the peasantry becoming more stationary than before. The consequence of this was, that the proprietors took up the idea of claiming a property in the land itself. Having the jurisdiction over the peasant, who could not marry without the proprietor's consent, allowed to flog, provided no wound was made, permitted to separate him from his family, and transport him to Siberia, the proprietors began to exact from him larger payments of produce, and also took into their own hands portions of the land which the peasant had formerly cultivated for his own use and means of living, and made him thenceforth till it for theirs.

The result of this was that the peasants, in the hope of bettering their condition, began to move from the estate of one proprietor to that of another, by whom they were always sure to be gladly received, and to be granted the use of a portion of land. But when war broke out, the proprietor, who was bound to bring a certain number of armed men for the service of his sovereign, often found himself unable to furnish the contingent which his sovereign had a right to demand from him, whilst the neighbouring proprietor, who had, perhaps, received a large accession of peasants, brought only the number which had been stipulated for at a period when his estate was scantily peopled.

To meet this state of affairs, in about the middle of the sixteenth century a nominal roll of householders on each estate was ordered to be made, and, at the same time, a law was declared by which the peasant was forbidden to leave the estate on which he was resident at the time such nominal roll was made, without previously obtaining the consent of his proprietor.

From this measure commenced the real serfdom of the Russian peasant, and the claim by the proprietor to the soil of the land; the peasant, however, during all that time, and down to 1861, claiming that he was by prescription, custom, and law entitled to a certain portion of the land as the means of subsistence for himself and his family; in fact, that between himself and the land there was a natural and inseparable connexion.

The dvorovi, or slaves, formed another class. In the wars against the Tartars, Finns, Poles, and others, many centuries ago, the prisoners taken in war were made slaves, but neither they nor their descendants ever held, or claimed to hold, land like the peasants, but rendered services in the house or on the land of their respective proprietors, receiving no wages, but being clothed and maintained. In addition to these prisoners of war, many of the native population, for the purpose of protecting themselves against the violence of the age in which they lived, sought protection at the hands of some powerful noble, and obtained it on voluntarily becoming his slaves, and agreeing that their descendants should be slaves also.

These dvorovi, or slaves, were not in any way mixed up with the peasants until the reign of Peter the Great. That sovereign ordered a general census to be taken of the whole population, and caused the proprietors to make a return in one list of the whole number of their peasants and dvorovi. Peter's intention and aim being, that out of the joint numbers of peasants and dvorovi he might make up a regular and standing army.

From this period the nobles were no longer compelled in time of war to bring with them and maintain a fixed number of men, but, instead thereof, to give periodically so many, whether peasants or dvòrovi, who were to become and remain regular soldiers. The proprietors were, however, compelled, in addition, to pay to the Crown a capitation tax in respect of the number of their peasants and dvorovi, and also to serve in the army, or in the civilian departments, during the pleasure of the sovereign, receiving payment according to rank.

By this measure the peasants lost to some extent their distinctive class, and became mixed up with, and treated as, the dvorovi; and in numerous instances the proprietors took some of their peasants from the land, and made them act as servants or slaves in their houses and on their estates. In 1858, however, these proceedings on the part of the proprietors were prohibited by law.

In February, 1861, the proprietors' peasants, exclusive of the Crown and monastic peasants, and of the dvorovi, numbered about twelve millions. They held more or less of the land, subject to the payment of an annual rent, and to the rendition of service, by unpaid labour. The amount of rent was not fixed by law, but depended solely on the will of the proprietor. There was, however, a law limiting the rendition of service to three days in a week. But this law was seldom observed by the proprietors, who exacted from the peasant as much unpaid labour as they required, leaving him to cultivate his land, upon which his whole means of subsistence depended, how and when he could. The peasant had no appeal, and no court to which he could apply for redress, and, as already stated, the proprietors could flog or transport him to Siberia. In this latter case, however, the peasant became free for ever from the jurisdiction of his proprietor, and at once received from the Crown the use of a sufficient quantity of land to cultivate.

Thus matters stood until 1861, and certainly, if the above picture of the state of the peasants be faithfully drawn, as in the main I believe it to be, their condition was such as to require a radical amelioration. This amelioration was not looming very far in the distance.

The Emperor had been for some time

"taking notes." He had submitted his wishes and intentions to the council, or assembly of nobles, and finally, in order to overcome the opposition he was encountering, presented himself one day before them, and stated in effect that as he governed Russia by his own sole will, that will should be exercised in the immediate abolition throughout his dominions of the existing serfdom and slavery.

Immediately afterwards the Emperor issued an ordinance, dated February 19, 1861, old style, by which he declared that both peasants and dvorovi should be free from the jurisdiction and power of the proprietors, and that they should have all the rights and privileges of free citizens, amenable only, like the rest of their fellow-subjects, to the laws of the Imperial Government.

To allow of the necessary arrangements

and provisions under the ordinance being satisfactorily carried out and completed, the services of the dvorovi, and some of the then existing obligations on the proprietors and peasants, were continued for a short period.

In conformity with the terms of the ordinance of February, 1861, and by mutual agreement between the dvorovi and their masters, the former might immediately become free, and in numerous instances their immediate freedom was granted, and accepted.

It was also declared by the ordinance of February that the proprietors should give up to the peasants, at a fixed annual rental, the land which they were then holding and cultivating, but in case it should exceed certain limits, regard being had to the number of peasants, the proprietors might resume the surplus.

The land so to be given up is to be placed at the disposition of each village or commune for allotment amongst its peasants, the whole body of the peasants of such village determining amongst themselves the allotment to, and the rental to be paid by, each.

The proprietors were ordered to hand to the justice of the peace of their respective districts, before the 19th of February, 1862, a deed, called a charter, setting out and defining the quantity and boundaries of the land so given up to each village, and specifying the amount of rental to be paid for it by such village. It appears that it has hitherto been the custom, and is still so to remain, that it is the village which holds the land, and is liable for the rent, and that the individual peasant is, so to say, merged in the general body of his commune. For instance, if one particular peasant does not pay his proportion of the general rent, the proprietor knows nothing about it. He looks to the village for the payment of the whole of his rent, and the head men of the village settle with the defaulting tenant. In White (Polish) Russia, and in Little Russia (the Ukraine), this system does not obtain, each peasant tenant being responsible for his own rental only, and not for the rental of the other tenants of his village.

If the proprietors failed to present the required deed, or charter, within the time prescribed, the justice of the peace had the power to define the land, and grant the charter in their names and at their expense.

All the arrangements respecting the land, its quantity, and rental, and all matters incident thereto, are to be determined, in the first instance, by the justice of the peace.

If his decision be objected to, either by proprietor or peasant, an appeal lies to the governor of the province, and his council or committee. All the charters must, under the ordinance, be finally settled and granted before the 19th of February, 1863, old style.

The justice of the peace is a new institution, and was founded for the purposes of carrying out the provisions of the ordinance. The annual pay of this officer is about 240*l.*, out of which he has to defray his travelling expenses, and the salary of his secretary. This pay does not appear very large, but the Government provides for his use a silver-gilt chain, which he may wear round his neck like the mayors of our municipalities, and which, perhaps, in some measure, compensates in the justice's mind for the want of the silver in his pocket.

Out of the land assigned by the proprietor

the peasant has the right of purchasing, without the consent of the proprietor, such portion of it as constitutes his *oussadba*, or homestead, consisting of the land on which stand his house, yard, and farm-buildings, comprising, perhaps, on an average, three-quarters of an English acre. Of course, I speak only of those I saw in one part of the country. The fixed price which the peasant must pay for this homestead is calculated at the rate of twenty-five roubles, or four pounds English, for each male person of his village—that is to say, that if there were one hundred males in his village, the peasant would have to pay for his homestead four pounds; if three hundred males, he would have to pay twelve pounds. I could not exactly understand, and am consequently unable to explain, the basis on which this assessment of value is made.

The remainder of the land can only be purchased by the village with the consent of the proprietor.

The ordinance, however, declares that the proprietors may demand, at any time after they have granted the charters, and so soon as such charters shall have been approved of by the proper authorities, the amount of the purchase-money of the whole of the land so granted, and the Government is thereupon bound to take the land and pay such purchase-money, less the sum of twenty pounds per centum. Up to the month of August, 1862, the Government had not been called upon to pay in this respect more than about five millions of roubles, or about two hundred thousand pounds English.

Of course, the ordinance of February, 1861, effects a complete revolution in the respective positions and rights of the proprietors, peasants, and dvorovi. It was not to be expected that so large and widely-extended a reform as this should have been received with unanimity. To the advanced and enlightened mind of the Emperor some such measure appeared necessary, and that powerful party which desires to see the onward progress and future welfare of the Russian people, warmly supported the Emperor's views. But that which is called the old Russian party is opposed to it. They urge that the measure will ruin the smaller proprietors; that there will be no labourers to hire for cultivating the land except at a cost which will be quite unremunerative to the hirer; that the peasants, as a rule, have not capital enough to work the soil to advantage; that the crops of all kinds will deteriorate in quantity and quality; that as the proprietors purchased their lands without any restriction, and hold in themselves the fee-simple of such lands, it becomes an act of confiscation to compel them now to give up a portion at a rental to be fixed by others; that the country is not ripe for so great an organic change; and, finally, they ask, "Why the Crown did not first free its own peasants?"

It seems to be admitted by the other side —that is to say, by those who support the Emperor's ordinance—that the smaller proprietors may possibly incur losses and inconveniences, but that as justice to the peasant and the general interests of the country demand an alteration in the existing laws, such alteration cannot be stopped or put aside by the continuance of a system which, however beneficial to the small proprietors, is a robbery and a gross injustice on the peasant; that the rate of labour will be regulated by the laws of supply and demand; that in their deeds the fee-simple of the land was not granted to the proprietors, and that the production of the deeds will prove it; and finally, that as the Crown peasant holds his land at a fixed rental, and yields no unpaid labour service, there was not the same pressing necessity of dealing with his case as there was in the instance of the proprietors' peasant.

It would be presumptuous in a foreigner who has not been three months in Russia to offer an opinion upon a subject of such magnitude; but one cannot help feeling that the answers are more valid than the objections, and that if Russia seeks to hold, as from her vast resources and the natural intelligence of her people she seems entitled to do, a prominent position amongst the civilised countries of the world, it was necessary that she should, as quickly as possible, put away from her the stain of that system of limited slavery which has so long prevailed, and which has obviously tended to harden the mind and feelings of the proprietor class, and to bow down the spirit, and subvert every growing idea of self-reliance and independence in the peasantry.

No doubt it will take many years to raise the Russian peasant from his present state of mental subjection to the standard of the English yeoman. Additional improvements must be effected, which time and experience will introduce. But it may be safely predicted that the Emperor's ordinance of the 19th of February, 1861, was the first step towards raising the peasant's social and material condition.

The peasant is now freed from the jurisdiction of his proprietor; he has no unpaid labour-service to render; he can purchase his homestead by a moderate payment; and he can hold his farm land at a fair, and, what to him is of the first importance, at a *fixed*, annual rental.

But, on the other hand, he has to free himself from the domination of superstition, and from his habits of idleness and intemperance.

The ordinance of February, 1861, does not, as intimated above, touch the position, or in any manner vary the status, of the peasants on the Crown or Government estates.

These in many instances hold to-day the same land which their fathers cultivated; they pay a fixed annual rental, but, unlike the proprietors' peasants, they cannot be called on to render any unpaid labour-service, so that the whole of their industry is for their own exclusive benefit. They cannot, however, quit their villages or communes without the previous consent of their fellow-villagers, because as the Crown looks to the village, and its inhabitants as a body, for its rent, so the village must, in its turn, look to the separate and collective industry of its inhabitants to make up the required annual rental. Should the land, however, be proved to have become deteriorated, the Crown gives other land in exchange.

It is said that an ordinance will be issued in the course of the coming year, regulating the status, and declaring the freedom, of the Crown peasant. One cannot but hope that this will be the case, seeing, amongst other things, that it will cut away from the grumblers the plausible objection they take in putting the question, "Why did not the Crown first free its own peasants?"

There is also another, though numerically speaking much smaller, class of peasants, called the appanage peasants, belonging to the reigning family. I understand that this class was formed by the Emperor Paul decreeing that certain of the Crown or Government estates should thenceforth be the private property of the reigning family, and that the late Emperor Nicholas, when urged to give up these appanaged estates, refused, on the ground that, as the form of government in Russia might some day be changed, it was right that the reigning family should be possessed of some private revenues and property over which the Government of the day shall have no power.

As the above subject commands attention in England, and as it is not always easy to procure reliable information, this plain and concise treatment of it may be found interesting to those who are unable by their avocations, or want of time, to acquire the information on the spot.

CHAPTER IV.

RUSSIAN BATHING—PUBLIC MEETING OF THE GOVERNOR AND PEASANTS — PEASANTS' FÊTE.

THE governor of the province arrived at my friend's house during our visit. His Excellency was on a tour of inspection through his government, principally connected with the absorbing question between the proprietor and peasant, and came for the purpose of holding a public meeting of the peasants of the three neighbouring communes.

Having heard in England and Germany no end of yarns about the Russian mode of bathing, which, by the way, I had always looked upon as a sort of traveller's story, and being told that, as this was Saturday, I might see this bathing with my own eyes, I determined to do so; so, having enlisted the gentlemen for the interesting expedition and exhibition, we betook ourselves in the evening to a sunny spot on the river's side to see what was to be seen. Four wooden huts were pointed out on the opposite side of the river, about two hundred yards up its bank, distinguishable from the other houses of the village principally by the marks of smoke over their entrance doors. Three of these huts were used by the men, and the other by the women; in them they lie down on a sort of wooden platform close to, and some part of it over, a large oven, which is made nearly red-hot, and upon and into which pails of cold water are from time to time thrown. The steam is thus got up to a pretty considerable extent, and the heat of course becomes very great. I subsequently tried one of these affairs, but found it impossible to remain much more than a minute. The peasants, however, endure the process for some twelve or fifteen minutes, striking themselves all the time with small branches of trees or shrubs, and rubbing, or rather scrubbing, their bodies with what they call Machalka. This is made from the inner bark of the birch-tree, cut up and shredded, and looking not unlike so much string; not that it feels like it, however, for its firmer quality gives it a scratching power, which effectually cleans the skin, and makes it tingle again.

Having used this for a time, they pass their hands over their limbs, peeling away, as it was described to me, the outer skin, by which I suppose is meant the accumulated impurities.

After they had been in these huts some twenty minutes, we saw the men, and the women too, running from them down the bank to the river, into which they threw themselves, remaining in the water about three minutes. They were all evidently of opinion that "beauty needs not the foreign aid of ornament," for they turned out in Nature's own buff, only instead of buff it was a pretty deep red, caused by the severity of the steaming process on their skins. I was told that in the winter, when the rivers are frozen, some of the men throw themselves into the snow; but from the answers to questions we asked of some of the peasants, I have reason to believe that very few amongst them do this, and that as a practice it does not exist. One man we spoke to shook his head, and said that he had done it once in his life—clearly meaning us to understand that he would not do it again, if he knew it.

The peasantry and humbler classes use this bath every Saturday, and occasionally on fête-days. Considering that their ablutions on the other days of the week may almost be represented by the word *nil*, and that on going to bed they only take off their boots or shoes, it would seem not unreasonable to suppose that they might require these occasional strong measures. Upon remarking to my friend on the unusual circumstance of men and women running about in a state of nudity in a public situation, with people passing by every minute, I was told that they are so innocently-minded that they do not give the matter a thought, and that the practice produces no immorality.

In conformity with the governor's wish, the peasants of the three communes met to-day on the lawn in front of the house, to the number of about two hundred and fifty. It was charming weather, and the scene very interesting. The costumes of the men in their different coloured shirts, worn outside the trousers and coming nearly down to the knee, were quite picturesque. A large semicircle was formed, into which the governor, attended by the justice of the peace ornamented with his gilt chain, advanced. The three mayors of the three communes, with their badges round their necks, stood in front. Behind them the starosta, with their badges; and behind these the arbitrators, or peasants' judges, chosen from among themselves; and behind these, again, the general body of the peasants. They all appeared very contented and well fed. I was told that nearly every one of them, for his station in life, was well off in this world's goods, and certainly, looking at their houses, their cattle, horses, carts, and granaries, I saw no reason to doubt the truth of the statement. Then the governor made them a speech, which must have been in effective language, if I might judge from the earnest manner in which they listened, and to which every now and then they gave an unanimous, though not noisy, assent. The manner of the speech was, however, a little marred to my English taste by the governor not being raised above his audience, and by his walking up and down during its delivery. Long before he had arrived at its termination, his hearers had congregated so closely around him, that I could not help exclaiming: "Though lost to sight, to memory dear!" This speech-making to open-air meetings is something new in Russia.

In the governor's oration, as explained to me—for being in the Russian language, of course I did not understand one word—his Excellency pointed out to his hearers the alterations which the ordinance of the 19th of February had effected in their status, told them that by the clemency and wisdom of their Emperor they had become free citizens —(cheers, as the reporters of the *Times* would have written, had they been present) —reminded them of their duties in their new positions, exhorted them to have their children taught to read and write, told them if they had any complaints to make against their justice of the peace to make them then and there; and finally inculcated on them the necessity of respecting the rights of property in others, as they would have their own rights respected and observed.

The last exhortation I believe to be very

necessary, for the following day we met one of them coming out of the forest with something that clearly did not belong to him, and I heard more than once that the observance of the good old principle of *meum* and *tuum* is not very strictly attended to amongst them. I was told that the chief question the priest asks of the lower orders, when they go to confession, is directed to the Eighth Commandment and its observance.

However, to go back to the meeting. Some of the peasants then asked questions bearing upon the points between the proprietors and themselves, and received answers with which they appeared perfectly contented. The governor then withdrew, the peasants formed themselves into knots, discussing all they had heard, and, after a time, went off to their homes.

It has been stated that in many parts of the country the peasant was much discontented with the proposed new settlement of the land question, having taken the idea into his head that the land was to be given to him for nothing, and being, therefore, greatly disappointed when he found that he had to buy his homestead, and pay rent for the land he cultivated.

I believe there was some foundation for this statement. I was told that some persons, for designs of their own, had instilled that idea into the mind of the peasant, in the hope that when he found it had no reality he would resort to acts of violence, which might afterwards be used against him, and against the scheme for his freedom.

At Kasan, for instance, where the peasants are alleged to have held that idea, they sought an interview, some twelve months ago, with the governor upon this subject.

Both parties, it is to be hoped, misunderstood one another, for the governor, instead of meeting the peasants, and explaining to them their position and their proprietors' rights, called out the troops to disperse them. It would not be just towards the governor to give the *ex parte* account I received of this matter at Nijni Novgorod, but the result was that some six or seven hundred of the unarmed peasants were killed or wounded.

A great deal was tried to be made out of this sad event to the disadvantage of the peasants, but the good sense and firmness of the Government prevailed, and the work of freedom and justice was not arrested.

In the evening our hostess gave a fête in an open part of the adjoining forest to the wives, sons, and daughters of the peasantry on the estate. The spot was admirably chosen, as, with her cultivated taste for the beautiful both in nature and art, it was sure to be. The scene was charming. A large piece of land with bright green turf, hemmed in by dark-coloured pine and fir trees, with overhead an almost Italian sky, was filled by the peasantry to the number of nearly three hundred. In the centre was a swing, upon which the juveniles were amusing themselves, and, round the outside of the circle, benches for the lookers-on.

The women—many of whom we had doubtless seen the preceding day taking the river in nature's uniform—were now dressed out in their holiday garments. Though crinolines have not yet become an institution among them, the evident signs of that fondness for dress which appears to prevail more or less (and a good deal more of the former than the latter) in the minds and hearts of all the daughters of Eve, in every country and of every condition, from the black lady of the Australian woods, adorned with red-ochre and white paint, to the high-born beauty of the London drawing-room, afforded sufficient proof that it was not the want of will, but rather the want of the material, which prevented these uncultivated daughters of Russia disporting themselves in all the stages of stiff petticoats, crinolines, or cages.

But the dresses. How shall I describe them? As my pen cannot do them full justice, I shall only say that they consisted, in some instances, of flowered damasks of every colour; in others, of velvets, which had some time or other cost no end of money, and of satins, which doubtless were quite the thing some eighty years ago, when Catherine Alexovina II. was empress. Most of these dresses were trimmed round the edges with gold fringe or gold borders. Over their shoulders they wore small shawls of very gay colours, whilst on their heads they wore handkerchiefs not very tastefully arranged. This handkerchief is a new feature in their costume. Formerly the unmarried women had no covering on their heads, but plaited their hair, and tied the ends with smart ribands, which hung gracefully over their shoulders. The married women wore a something between a cap and a turban, concealing their hair entirely. I saw this head-dress afterwards in St. Petersburg upon a rather pretty nurse, and thought it extremely becoming. How it would have looked on an ugly woman—if there is such a thing—I am not prepared to say. However, since the peasants in our hostess's part of the world have become free, they have all adopted the handkerchief, fancying that that costume brought them somewhat nearer in equality to their superiors in rank. And so the world wags on. Progress is the order of the day, and whether it takes the form of a six-pound franchise, or a change in a Russian peasant woman's head-dress, the principle is pretty much the same.

The fête began with the women forming themselves to the number of about one hundred into a circle, and moving round by a sort of one-two step to the music of a slow dirge-like chant. There was not much animation, and it was difficult to imagine what particular amusement they derived from the operation. The governor took me into the middle of this circle, from which we had a full view of the performers. Truth compels me to say that out of the whole lot of them I did not see half a dozen faces which could be called pretty. But then it must be borne in mind that they were all hardworking people, whose avocations took them from morning to night, summer and winter, into the open air, exposed four months in the year to a burning sun, and for the other eight months to all kinds of changeable weather, some of it very cold indeed.

After the circle-dance had gone on for some time, another smaller one within it was formed, consisting of about fourteen men and women, all supposed to be related one to the other. After a few preliminaries, one of the men advanced, leading out one of the women. After going through several ceremonious steps and figures, he presented her with a handkerchief, kissed her three times, and returned her to her place. This woman was the mother of one of the younger ones in the circle, and as she had received the handkerchief, and had not objected ostensibly to the kisses, the man was emboldened to lead out the daughter. The couple then went through many steps and captivating figures, now advancing, and then bashfully retiring. At last the man dropped the fatal handkerchief which was to decide his lot, and, of course, the girl, like most other girls in all parts of the world, seeking an establishment of their own, picked it up quickly and presented it to her future *caro sposo*, whereupon the kissing, that pleasant heart's language of all countries, was very liberally, and this time more ardently, administered to the young lady, who, I must say, received and returned it in a very generous spirit, notwithstanding the publicity of the locale. And so the betrothal of this couple was completed. A liberal distribution of whisky all round by our kind-hearted hostess seemed to be as much relished by the dancers as the kissing had been by the select few, and so that ceremony was finished.

Our indefatigable hostess then distributed to the general company whisky, cakes, apples, and other sweetmeats, as Paddy would say. Fireworks were let off, and holiday dresses taken off. These latter the women packed up in their head-handkerchiefs, and, as the "shades of evening *did* close o'er us," we all returned to our respective homes, the peasants wakening up the dull old forest with their monotonous songs and merry laughter.

One could not but be struck with pleasure, and some astonishment too, at the quiet, gentle manners and innate good breeding of this concourse of men, women, and children of the real working class of Russian villages.

The élite of the villagers, however, did not show on the occasion, thinking, I suppose, that their dignity might suffer by *too* close a contact with the masses, for even the peasantry have their own aristocrats among them.

CHAPTER V.

A WOLF-HUNT—RUSSIAN LEAVE-TAKING—A PEASANT'S TEA-PARTY.

As the governor wished to have a wolf-hunt, the gentlemen started early on the following morning for a neighbouring village, the peasants of which had been invited to assist. From the village we made for a forest not very far off. Our party consisted altogether of about forty-eight men, one-half of whom was armed with guns and rifles. The governor and I carried a sort of short pitchfork in case of coming to close quarters with the enemy, the idea of which, when first presented to my mind, gave me a sort of what old women call "all-overishness." A couple of country carts to carry the commissariat, and the never-failing stone jars of whisky, brought up the rear. On entering the forest, the carts, with their drivers and horses, were encamped in an "oasis," to await our return. Leaving these, we marched forward in single file, making no more noise than absolutely necessary. After a short advance the knowing ones found and pointed out the fresh tracks of the game of which we were in search, whereupon the gunners and riflemen were posted two and two at intervals of about one hundred and fifty yards in the proximity of the spot for which it was supposed the wolves would make after their quarters had been beaten up. The governor and I were stationed together, with the promise that before the "beating up" began we should have a good rifle marksman to support us. The rest of the party, armed with long sticks and stout poles, were then told off towards the rear of the forest, and formed in a line directly opposite to us, about three-quarters of a mile off.

As soon as these arrangements had been made, the captain of the party, a tall, weather-beaten, elderly peasant, who put one in mind of Cooper's "Leather-Stocking," came back to where the governor and I were posted, and, taking his stand between us, put his hands before his mouth, and, lowering his head down to the earth, began a most unearthly howl, gradually raising his head, meanwhile, until he attained his erect position. This howl, we were afterwards assured, was an exact imitation of the wolf's, and was the signal to the bush-beating party, who were thereupon to advance on our line, beating the woods and halloaing to drive the wolves before them and upon us. Our captain then told us to stand firm and not to speak, whilst he himself stood, rifle in hand, ready for the fun. The governor brought his pitchfork to "the present," and, not to be behindhand, I followed suit.

Very soon we heard the voices of the advancing party becoming gradually more and more distinct. Our captain was looking serious and somewhat excited, when, after a few more minutes, crack went the report of a rifle considerably to the left of our position. Then the voices of the men became less and less distinct, and shortly afterwards our captain threw his rifle into the hollow of his arm, and gave vent to some speech, which, from his manner, I thought did not convey a blessing. A few minutes more elapsed, when he said, rather sulkily, that matters had gone wrong. Eventually the outsiders straggled in, and reported that five wolves had shown the whites of their teeth, broken through the extreme end of our line to the left, and escaped for that day; one of them being wounded by the shot we had heard. There was no help for it. The forest was of enormous extent, and it was too late to look for any more tracks. So we made our own tracks back to the "oasis," where we had planted our commissariat, leaving the brutes to exult over their victory, and go through another hard winter in that swampy, desolate forest, to which I should think that death by one of our unsportsmanlike pitchforks would have been preferable.

Nothing daunted, however, by our bad luck in the field, or rather in the forest, we enjoyed a capital lunch, the peasants, as usual, doing due honour to the contents of the whisky-jar. Some fair rifle-practice wound up the day's amusement, at which the prize was carried off by a good-looking young fellow, who seemed quite proud of his performance, and as the wind had now become very cold and cutting, we hastened off as fast as our horses could carry us to our friend's comfortable house and hospitable table.

On the following morning, his Excellency, being obliged to return to his seat of government, took leave in what I was informed was the regular Russian mode. Having ascertained that all was ready for his departure, the governor came into the drawing-room where we were all assembled, and took his seat, silence being observed by all present. A few minutes having elapsed, he rose and crossed himself. This is the signal for leave-taking. Every one then rose, and the adieus were made. We accompanied him to the door, where we found his carriage waiting with six post-horses; the drivers had ornamented their hats with flowers and peacocks' feathers in his Excellency's honour. The peacock's feather is very much in vogue with this class, but is rarely sported except on special occasions.

On my friend's estate—and I believe it is the same on all large estates—there is a superintendent, who is called the starosta. This starosta was a fine-looking old peasant, with a long white beard flowing down his breast, and, although seventy-six years of age, still hale and active, and very intelligent. He was determined that the English visitors to his master should take tea with him at his house in one of the adjoining villages, so we set off with our hostess and some other visitors in an open dos-à-dos carriage, capable of holding ten persons, drawn by four horses abreast. We flew along à la Russe down one little hill and up another at an astonishing pace, and arrived at the old man's dwelling about three o'clock in the afternoon. Although not understanding five words of the Russian language—and of course he understood no other—yet when he placed his arm within mine and showed me his house, land, and outbuildings, and explained different matters connected with them, I understood pretty well, from his intonation and the signs he used, what he intended to convey to me. Some may, perhaps, think that I only imagined I understood him; at all events, I believed at the time that I did, and that was half the battle won.

After spending some time looking over the out-door arrangements, we returned to one of the upper rooms in the house, where tea, fresh cucumbers, honey, and whisky, with good bread-and-butter, were profusely administered to us, our hostess having the seat of honour under the holy image. We got through easily enough with the tea, and the cucumbers spread with honey, but the whisky at half-past three in the afternoon was trying. As the rest of the guests were ladies, I had to sacrifice myself to save them; so I tossed off the contents of a good-sized wine-glass of this whisky to the starosta's health, with many misgivings, however, as to the results. I fear I did not secure so much respect from him as I should have done had I drank the contents of a second glass, which he had poured out as a stirrup-cup, but which I could not screw myself up to attempt.

On parting, the starosta's nephew made a little speech, which, being afterwards interpreted, I learned, conveyed that he was not very rich in this world's goods, but all he had he was ready to give me. Of course this was merely intended as the usual compliment, and I mention it only as one of the many instances I came across of the somewhat Eastern character and modes of expression of the Russian peasant. I may add, for the benefit of any of my countrymen who may be driven to a glass of whisky in Russia in the early afternoon, that whether it was attributable to the drive home, or to the sharp air of the country, no anticipated headache followed.

A few days after this it happened to be

the name-day of the major-domo of the establishment, and as that day is always kept by those of his class with great solemnity, and much eating and drinking, we were invited to his house at one o'clock, whither in due course we proceeded with our hostess and her other friends.

The major-domo took his seat at the table, whilst his sons and daughters waited on us. The board was covered with sugared cakes and fresh and preserved fruits, whilst a sparkling wine from the Crimea did duty for champagne, which it pretty much resembles. It is not so dear as the veritable champagne, which costs in Russia about 10*l.* a dozen, whereas the Crimean wine may be had for about 2*l.* a dozen. The latter, of course, is not liable to duty, whilst the former is charged in that respect to the amount of about 40s. a dozen.

CHAPTER VI.

TOWN OF SALZI—MORNING VISIT TO A RUSSIAN MERCHANT—NOVGOROD THE GREAT—THE RIVER VOLCHOW—RAILROAD TO MOSCOW.

Having enjoyed the unbounded hospitality of our friends almost longer than we thought right, and seen as much as we could of the interior country life of a Russian family, we made our arrangements to proceed across the country to Novgorod Welike (Novgorod the Great), and down the river Volchow to Volkoffskaia, where we might take the train to Moscow. We had received an invitation to stop on our way at a small town called Salzi, and pay a visit to a Russian flax-merchant resident there. We arrived at his house about half-past eleven in the forenoon, and were received by the gentleman and his handsome wife with the same hospitality that marked all classes in Russia with whom we came in contact. As our friends, however, could not speak any language but their own, our conversation and compliments were necessarily carried on through the medium of our hostess, who had accompanied us so far on our journey to Novgorod. We were shown into a splendid suite of seven rooms, all elegantly and tastefully furnished. A servant soon entered, bearing a tray with tumblers of champagne, première qualité. One might well be excused wishing, as he sipped a tablespoonful of it, that it was seven o'clock in the evening instead of half-past eleven in the forenoon. Drinking champagne, however good, "before," as Jack says, "the sun is over the foreyard-arm," is a thing not to be done, let your hostess's eyes be ever so bright. The champagne was succeeded by the inevitable tea, to which we did, as usual, ample justice.

We explored the town, which contains about four thousand inhabitants. There was not much to interest a stranger. Good wide streets, and a navigable river, by which the flax is sent with other produce to St. Petersburg for shipment to England.

On our way to Salzi we passed a picturesque-looking church perched on a little hill, one side of which had gradually disappeared, until it almost seemed as though the building had no foundations, and only received its support from two enormous beams by which it was shored up. On the other side is a coloured sketch of it, made on the spot by our obliging hostess.

After some hours' bumping over more sand-hills, we arrived at Novgorod Welike in the evening. It is a curious old town, quite unlike any we had previously seen, and is one of the oldest in Russia, having been founded as early as the fifth century. It is situated on the river Volchow, by which it has communication with St. Petersburg, and the governments or provinces on the river Volga. For a long distance before it is reached the traveller sees the gilded domes of its numerous churches, from which he supposes that it is a much larger place than it really is. It formerly possessed a numerous population, and was the seat of many manufactures. Like Pskoff, however, it suffered by the foundation of St. Petersburg, and its trade and commerce visibly declined. Its population now is only a little over eighteen thousand, of whom seventeen thousand belong to the Greek Church. There is one Protestant and one Catholic church here. The Kremlin is the most remarkable part of Novgorod. It was built by Vladimir in 1044, and was, like other fortresses, used as an asylum for safety in time of war. It is still surrounded by high battlemented walls, and the high road from St. Petersburg to Moscow now passes through its centre. As a fortress at the present day I imagine it would be useless. Within its walls are the official residence of the governor, the cathedral of Saint Sophia, six other churches, and the palace of the Archmandrite, corresponding in rank with our archbishops.

The cathedral was also built by Vladimir, and has been several times restored, the last time in 1839, when great pains were taken to preserve the old style of architecture, and to restore the old paintings and mosaics. In it is the coffin of St. Ivan of Novgorod, and it is further famous for its bronze doors, which are eleven feet high, and covered with figures.

There is also a church dedicated to St. Joachem and St. Anne, which is worth a visit, and is said to be the first church which was built here at the period of the introduction of Christianity in 989 for the first bishop of Novgorod.

In the trading part of the town is a place called the Court of Jaroslaw, after one of the reigning families, remarkable chiefly for its historical legends. Jaroslaw granted a charter to the inhabitants, by which the independence of Novgorod was established under a republican form of government, and to this court the great bell summoned the inhabitants for the election of the Possodniki, or Presidents, who, upon their election, were bound to take an oath on the cross to preserve the charter, which, if they attempted to infringe, led to their being brought back again to this court, and tried for their acts.

John the Third, surnamed the Terrible, who seems to have earned his unenviable title by all sorts of horrible cruelties, though not to have been quite such a ruffian as his grandson John the Fourth, who also obtained the same sobriquet, upset the charter granted by Vladimir, incorporated the town and province into his own dominions, and, much to the disgust of the superstitious Novgorodians, walked off with the palladium of their liberties, their great bell, and had it hung up in the Kremlin at Moscow, where it was pointed out to us when we visited that city.

During the summer there is a large concourse of travellers, and a considerable trade carried on in corn, wheat, salt, flax, cloth, iron, wood, and other productions.

At about forty English miles distant is a small town, Staraia Russa, with a population of about six thousand inhabitants, famous for its mineral waters, possessing nearly the same qualities, it is said, as those at Kreuznach, in Rhenish Prussia, and to which numbers betake themselves in the season. It is here that the salt is made for supplying the provinces of Novgorod and Twer.

Tradition has it that it was in Novgorod that the first Russian money was coined at the end of the fourteenth century, under Basil the Second. Up to that period they say that the inhabitants used skins of the marten and other wild animals as the circulating medium.

I imagine that a skin won in the chase from the grey back of a marten would have passed current for value more readily in those coinless times than a greenback of Mr. Federal Chase would do in these days. Still, to give every one his due, it must be admitted that when it came to quantities, the spoils of the American Chase are easier to carry in the pocket than those of the Russian one would have been; and that is about all that can be said in favour of the former.

We went to see the memorial monument which has been erected to commemorate the millennium of the foundation of Novgorod, and which the Emperor intends to inaugurate. Unfortunately it was covered up, and we could not see it: we heard that it was cast in bronze by the English company at St. Petersburg, and is very emblematic.*

According to Russian history, this town was originally governed as a republic, but its neighbours, being of a warlike and aggressive temperament, were in the habit of making frequent raids on it, until, in the ninth century, the Novgorodians called to

* I have, since my return, seen a beautiful copy of this monument, cast in bronze, in a reduced size, by the same company, for a friend of mine. It is the only copy in England, and a most interesting work.

Vincent Brooks, lith.

CARPENTER.

their assistance one Prince Rurik, stated to have been of Scandinavian birth, who, with his descendants, protected them so well, that in the course of time the Novgorodians absorbed the neighbouring states, until in its turn Novgorod was absorbed into the principality of Moscow, in 1477. For a short time, before Kieff became the capital, it is stated to have been the seat of the Russian Government. The stone and iron bridge crossing the Volchow river is a handsome edifice, though perhaps to English taste a little overdone with gilding and imperial eagles. There is a theatre, which, judging only from its exterior, is not a very spacious one, numerous hotels with unpronounceable names, and a very good public garden, in which a military band plays in the evening, and which, when we visited it, was crowded. Here, a little to our surprise, we met with that horrid pork-pie hat, which seems to be in great favour with the fashionable female world of Novgorod, but which we had hoped was a specialty only to be seen at some English watering-places. The streets were full of people, owing, perhaps, to its being market-day. Steamers ply from here to Volkoffskaia and to Kazan. The Alexander Nevskoi monastery in St. Petersburg is named after Prince Alexander Nevskoi, who ruled over Novgorod in the thirteenth century, and who defeated the Swedes in 1240 at the confluence of the Neva and Ishora, the place on which St. Petersburg now stands. It was from that victory that Alexander obtained the surname of Nevskoi, and it was in his honour that Peter the Great instituted the order of knighthood of St. Alexander Nevskoi in 1703.

After a few hours' steaming down the Volchow, we arrived at Volkoffskaia. This river, which issues from the great lake Ilmen, and flows into the Ladoga canal, is about twelve hundred feet in width at its broadest part, and in the summer carries large numbers of the clumsiest-looking craft. On either side are almost countless monasteries, convents, and churches. The selection of the land on which these buildings stand reflects credit on the taste and knowledge of value of those who made it. Whenever one of these buildings was passed, a great amount of crossing themselves took place among the passengers on the steamboat. They must have been tired of it at last, as the churches near Volkoffskaia received no attention at all, which was rather hard on them. Although on the sides of the river there were a few low hills, occupied by the monasteries, still the country presented an uninteresting surface, with little to arrest the tourist's attention. The fare by the steam-boat was very moderate.

At Volkoffskaia we took the train to Moscow. The time allowed for performing the journey between that city and St. Petersburg is twenty hours. It might easily be done in twelve. We were told that the Buffet interest is very strong on this line, and that great resistance is made to any shortening of the eating and drinking hours as at present established. However, it is said that with the new year will come the shortening of the journey to fourteen hours. Twelve months ago it took twenty-five hours. This line of railroad is, barring the wasted time, exceedingly well ordered, and the carriages most comfortable. They are fitted up with a great regard to the convenience and ease of the passengers, who, except for eating and drinking, need not quit them during the journey, however long. In the winter a stove is introduced into what are called the saloon carriages. The station-houses where the buffets are held exceed in size and tastefulness of arrangement anything of a similar kind we had previously seen. To English ideas the cost of the provisions appears large; still their quality, and the superior way in which they are put on the table, must be taken into account. It is stated that at each of these buffets a regular professed cook is kept. From personal observation, I should say that the Russians are the best eaters going. One of them told us quite seriously that what was absolutely necessary for a Russian would kill a German. And I can vouch from personal observation, that the

Germans are not to be laughed at for their prowess at table. Although the intervals between the buffets do not generally exceed more than four hours, still the Russian traveller is always ready for the attack. In order to give timely notice of starting of the train, a bell is rung with a one-two to tell you to prepare for your departure. At this signal the timid and the nervous hurry off to take their seats. The strong-minded of both sexes wait until the third bell sounds, and then are very often obliged to perform a sort of gymnastic operation to secure their carriages, which in the case of the stiff-petticoated ones causes some display to the amusement of the male looker-on.

It would really be better did ladies, when on a journey, discard these garments. In Switzerland it is no uncommon occurrence to see them going over the mountains with their hoops tied up, and slung on one of the pommels of the side-saddle, all ready for use the moment they descend from their mules, as if their reputations depended on not being without them. If ladies could only sometimes "see themselves as others see them," I think that their inherent delicacy would make them discard these very *discovering* inventions. In the drawing-room, and perhaps in walking, when they are well managed by the wearers, these hoops, no doubt, do set off the female dress, though they cause it frequently to catch fire, and conceal the proportions of the figure, which, after all, is a questionable matter of taste, but, when worn on journeys, are neither becoming to the wearers nor convenient to their neighbours.

CHAPTER VII.

ARRIVAL AT MOSCOW—MOSCOW—THE HOLY GATE — PROCESSION OF PRIESTS — THE KREMLIN—VIEWS—THE IBERIAN VIRGIN.

We arrived at Moscow at eight o'clock in the morning, not much fatigued, after sixteen hours in the railway. Before we had finished our travelling, we became accustomed to the long sederunts in the railway carriages, thinking nothing of passing three nights out of six in them.

We proceeded in search of the hotel called in Bradshaw's Continental Railway Guide "Laodies." The real name of this hotel is, or rather was, "Labadie;" which made all the difference in inquiring for it, and did not certainly tend, as we found, to facilitate the search for it.

However, for the guidance of those who may hereafter visit Moscow, and wish to look for this hotel, it may be mentioned that it is now called "Loubienka, ci-devant Labadie;" and a very good hotel it is, pleasantly situated in one of the best streets, and standing back on its own ground. We paid fifteen shillings a day for a sitting-room, two bedrooms, and ante-room, on the first-floor. The landlord and his wife are French, and intelligent, obliging people. The cuisine is undeniably good, and not very expensive.

Moscow, called in the Russian language Moskwa, is situated on the banks of a river of that name, and was for a long period prior to 1703 the capital of the Russian Government, but in that year Peter the Great transferred the seat of government to St. Petersburg. The form of the city is that of an irregular rhomboid, and its outside wall is said to be nearly twenty-six English miles in length, but it must be borne in mind that within it there are many public and private gardens, walks, and parks, which are laid out with great taste, and constitute a very pleasant feature of this great city.

Moscow appears to have undergone some rough treatment in its time. Three hundred years ago, the Tartars twice sacked and then burned it; on the last of which events it is said that nearly one hundred thousand persons perished by fire and sword. Then came accidental conflagrations, destroying large portions of the city; whilst in the early half of the seventeenth century, the

Poles, who seem at various times to have been very troublesome to the Russians, captured Moscow, laid a great part of it in ashes, and retained possession of it for three or four years. In 1812, the inhabitants set fire to it, by way of making things unpleasant to Napoleon I., who had calculated on passing the winter within its walls.

The Kremlin is in the centre of Moscow. It is surrounded with walls, from fifteen to eighteen feet thick, with towers and five gates, of which latter, one is called the Holy Gate, or Gate of the Saviour, in consequence of the picture of Our Saviour placed over it, and which is *said*, and the inhabitants believe, to have been painted by St. Luke. Every one on passing under this gate, and for about ten yards afterwards, must take off his hat. The first time we drove under it, the stupid courier did not tell us that it was the Holy Gate, and I sat composedly with my hat on as usual.

We had not gone, however, two or three yards, when our coachman, looking back, saw me with my head covered, and began such a series of contortions of body and face that I felt there must be something wrong, and so uncovered just in time to escape the eye of the sentry placed there to secure obedience to the regulation, and to save myself the annoyance of being sent back.

I only recovered my equanimity by heartily abusing the courier, who, I believe, purposely kept me in ignorance of the fact that I was passing under the gate of gates.

We were unsuccessful in obtaining access to the Cathedral of the Assumption, which is stated to have been founded in 1326, and to be the most splendid among the many splendid churches in Moscow. It is in this cathedral that the Russian sovereigns are crowned. Within the Kremlin walls there are upwards of thirty cathedrals and churches.

There is also the magnificent tower or belfry of Ivan Velike, and near its base, on a pedestal, the great bell of Moscow, cast in the reign of the Empress Anne. There is a large piece out of it, by which the visitor is better enabled to judge of its enormous thickness. This bell is said to weigh upwards of four hundred thousand pounds of English weight, and that whilst being cast, the religious feelings of the people were so excited, that those who had the means threw pieces of gold and silver into the burning mass. On the outside of it is a female figure, supposed to represent the

Empress, and beneath is a border of flowers. It is held in great veneration by the people.

Under the western walls of the Kremlin is a very pleasant public garden, which is much resorted to by the inhabitants of that quarter of the town, and which was brilliantly illuminated during our visit on the night of the Emperor's fête.

We had been told, when at Moscow, to ask for a species of white bread called kalatch, for which that city has for centuries been famous. It is made in the shape of a flat hand-basket, and, when eaten hot with lots of butter, reminds an English stomach of a married muffin and crumpet. In Moscow there are about one hundred and twenty vendors of this article. A fellow-traveller on the railroad told us that whenever he went to Moscow in the winter he took back to St. Petersburg a supply of this bread, hanging it out of the window to freeze.

We found that the Emperor was here, and in the evening there was a grand military illumination at the camp, about two miles out of the town. There was a long line of blazing tar-barrels, extending for six versts, sky-rockets, roman-candles, and every description of fireworks. The crowd was immense, and the Emperor was present in a tent in the centre of the camp.

Moscow contains a population of 320,000, 240 parish churches, 33 other churches and chapels, and 21 monasteries and convents. About ten years ago a new church of vast dimensions, dedicated to Our Saviour, was commenced, and is now nearly finished.

As a place of residence, many prefer Moscow to St. Petersburg, the climate of the former being more equal, and not so much exposed to strong winds and storms; but its badly-paved streets would be found a considerable drawback by the inhabitant of London or Paris. In driving through them, any attempt at conversation is out of the question, unless your companion has the lungs of a Stentor, and you have your ears very wide open. At Moscow there is no tariff for the hackney-carriages, which some people tell you is in the interest of the public, and that they get better served without one. To those who can speak the language, and who know the distances, this may be so, but it may be doubted whether it is the case as regards the travelling public. We paid, after the usual preliminary wrangle, five shillings for a miserable two-horse affair from the station to the hotel, a distance of about a mile—our luggage going in some other conveyance, for which, of course, we had to pay in addition.

Here we saw a tremendous procession of priests. One of the two Archbishops of Moscow was going to mass, accompanied by nearly two hundred ecclesiastics, besides men bearing banners and images, machines that looked for all the world like small square four-post bedsteads adorned with white silk curtains, other machines that resembled small round temples, the contents of which, whatever they were, were concealed by red curtains drawn closely round; and other contrivances, of which the names were unlearnable, and the description difficult. The mounted gendarmes in their light-blue uniforms; the priests, with their long, wild-looking hair hanging down their backs, and enormous beards flowing over their breasts, looking not over-clean, decked out in robes of all the colours of the rainbow, and of some colours, too, which the rainbow has not, and worked in gold and silver thread, presented a tout ensemble not to be seen, perhaps, in any other country; whilst the bareheaded crowds that lined the streets and followed the procession afforded unmistakable evidence, by their earnest and respectful demeanour, that they *felt* their religion in a greater degree than did some of the priests, who were laughing in no very decorous manner, even while intoning in public the services of their Church.

There can be no doubt that Moscow presents an infinity of subjects of stirring interest to the traveller. On an inspection of the visitors' book at the palace in the Kremlin, we saw the names of numerous

English people; and now that the railroad is open in its whole length from Berlin to St. Petersburg, and thence to Moscow, and every facility afforded to the tourist, it is probable that large numbers of our countrymen, and countrywomen too, will avail themselves of the opportunities afforded of visiting this remarkable city.

The vast treasures and curiosities in the palace in the Kremlin do not, perhaps, impress the mind so powerfully at the moment as they do after you have quitted them, and when the memory reverts to them.

A certain feeling of annoyance obtained with us at the way in which we were hurried over the inspection of objects on which we should have liked to dwell. A servant in livery accompanies the visitors in their progress through the building, and upon his tastes they are altogether dependent.

For instance, there is a whole-length portrait of Catherine II., in military uniform, on horseback. True, as a work of art it is not first rate, and the lady is riding en cavalier, which at this day is not the fashion as it was in hers; still, as the likeness of a once great and powerful sovereign—somehow or other we felt that it must be a faithful likeness—it was natural that we should have wished to study it. No time, however, was allowed for this, whilst in the next room we should have been allowed to waste a quarter of an hour in inspecting a great ugly pair of jack-boots, made with his own hands by Peter the Great; a curious relic, no doubt, as the work of imperial hands, but not worth, in that museum, more than a passing look. By our attendant, however, those boots were evidently a venerated institution. The jewelled crowns and splendid helmets of former ages and conquered countries were simply pointed out, as the attendant continued his walk, as the crown of a sovereign, or the helmet of some warrior whose name it was difficult to catch, and impossible, in the rapid succession of nomenclature, to retain in the memory. We got a glimpse, and that was all, of the crown of Poland, which is of polished gold, quite plain, with a cross on its top, and the crown of Vladimir II., of filigree gold, ornamented with pearls and precious stones, and which was used at the coronation of the Czars, until Peter the Great took it into his head to have a new fashioned one—which we afterwards saw at St. Petersburg. There was just sufficient time afforded to allow of the visitor wishing to examine all these things, when he was hurried off to some piece of gilded upholstery which had served as the throne at the coronation of some recent sovereign, whilst of the valuable gifts which Sultans and Princes had presented hardly a glimpse could be obtained. Whole ranges of apparently magnificent and curiously-inlaid weapons, arranged on the walls for inspection, were passed without a word of explanation or chance of examination. There was the chair in which Charles XII. is said to have been carried from the battle of Pultava, when he had his leg wounded by a shot, and also the state carriages of former sovereigns, with Anna Petrovna's curious garden-chair and Napoleon's travelling-carriage, which would have been passed by in the same scrambling manner, had we not pulled short up and insisted on asking whose they had been. The whole affair was evidently considered a confounded bore by the attendants, who did not, however, forget to put in their claims for "buckshcesh." Of all the nuisances which attend the sight-seer none is so objectionable as the professional showman. The absence of this animal constitutes one of the many charms of the Uffizzi and Pitti Palaces at Florence. There the visitor ranges at will up and down the long galleries unattended and unquestioned, and without being called upon to pay a penny. What a pity it is that the same course cannot be adopted in England and other countries. Let the servants stand about in the rooms to take care that no one improperly meddles with the objects exhibited; and let the visitor pay, if deemed necessary, on entrance, a capitation fee, to be divided amongst the attendants, leaving him free to devote as much of his time as he chooses to examining and studying the treasures and curiosities exhibited to his view.

Though not attempting to give a detailed description of Moscow, we may direct the attention of the traveller to the Foundling Hospital, the Riding-school, the University, and the Post-office; also to the statues in honour of Pojarski and Minnin in the Krasnoi-Ploschad, or the Red Place, which were erected by Alexander I. in commemoration of their having delivered the country from the invasion of the Poles in 1613. These statues are of bronze, and nearly fourteen feet high, and stand on a block of red granite, on which is an inscription in Russian and a bas-relief, the whole surrounded by a handsome iron railing. This monument is well worthy of examination. It represents Minnin appealing to the Prince to put himself at the head of the people and attack the Poles.

It was on their expulsion in that year that Michael Romanoff, alleged to have been descended in the female line from Rurik, mounted the throne of Russia, and became the founder of the present dynasty. In a court close to the Treasury are rows of cannon taken by the Russians at various times, a large proportion of which consists of those captured from the French in their retreat from Moscow in 1812. Prussia and Poland contribute their share, as does, in fact, nearly every nation under the sun excepting England.

The views of Moscow from the Kremlin-terrace, and also from the Seminoff monastery and the Sparrow-hill, are the best that can be obtained. It was on the Sparrow-hill that Napoleon obtained his first view of it, and counted those chickens which were not to be hatched.

We ascended the tower of the Seminoff

monastery, and obtained, as we thought, the best view of the city, which was spread out before us like an enormous panorama. The principal features in it are the Kremlin, with its painted towers and gilt cupolas, the lofty campanile of Ivan Velike, and the church of St. Basil, with its gaudy Eastern roofs; whilst behind and around the scene are long lines of white walls and buildings, presenting a curious contrast to the many coloured buildings within their circle. It was a novel circumstance that, at this tower, the lay brother who pointed out to us the different buildings in Moscow should have been totally blind. The way in which he rushed up and down the winding staircase was something wonderful, and it was not until we had been on the platform for some minutes asking questions and receiving answers as to this and that church, that we discovered the poor man was blind. It sounded strange when he subsequently told our interpreter that a great many English had been up the tower, and that he was always so glad to *see* them. Under the Sparrow-hill, across the river, is a convent for les demoiselles; but our guide informed us that none are admitted unless they are very rich. It is charmingly situated, though rather low, perhaps, and is well out of the noise and bustle of the city.

It has been previously stated that the Russian peasants attach great importance to their images or pictures; but there is one in Moscow, besides that supposed miraculous one over the Holy Gate leading out of the Red Place into the Kremlin, which is imagined to possess wonderful qualities. We did not see it, but were informed that this image or picture of the Virgin is never taken out of its chapel unless in a carriage with eight horses, and that upon the illness of the late Emperor Nicholas, when it was wished to try what effect it would have in restoring his Majesty's health, the image demonstrated in some way or other that it did not choose to make the journey, and so, as our informant said, "The Emperor died next day." It does seem difficult of belief that any Church should, in the nineteenth century, keep a carriage and horses for a picture. I thought at first that my informants were playing on my credulity in this matter, but subsequent inquiries, conducted, of course, with as much delicacy as possible, compel me to believe that the fact is as represented.

Since the foregoing appeared in *Bentley's Miscellany*, a friend has sent the following account of this image and her chapel, which he says is in a book by Kohl, an eminent writer on Russia, and Russian life:

"Her chapel consists of one undivided area, the saint herself being in a kind of sanctuary hollowed out at the farther end; here, in the half-darkened background, she may be indistinctly discerned, resplendent, however, in gold and precious stones. Her complexion, like that of all Russian saints, is dark brown, not to say black. Round her head is a net of real pearls; on one shoulder a large jewel is fastened, and another of equal brilliancy rests on her brow, above which glitters a brilliant crown. In one corner of the picture, on a silver plate, is inscribed *ἡ μήτηρ Θεοῦ τῶν Ἰβερῶν.*

"Around the picture are gold brocaded hangings, to which angels' heads, painted on porcelain with silver wings, are sewn;

whilst the whole is lighted up by thirteen silver lamps. Beside the picture there are a number of drawers containing wax tapers, and books having reference to her history. Her hand and the foot of the child are covered with dirt from the abundant kissing: it sits like a crust in little raised points, so that long since it has not been hand and foot that have been kissed; but the concrete breath of pious lips. The doors of the chapel stand open the whole day, and all are admitted who are in sorrow and heavy laden; and this includes here, as everywhere else, a considerable number, and the multitudes that stream in testify the power which this picture exercises over their minds. None ever pass, however pressing their business, without bowing and crossing themselves: the greater part enter, kneel devoutly down before 'the

Mother,' and pray with fervent sighs. Here come the peasants early in the morning before going to market, who lay aside their burdens, pray awhile, and then go their ways; hither comes the merchant on the eve of a new speculation, to ask the assistance of 'the Mother:' hither come the healthy and the sick, the wealthy and those who would become so; the arriving and the departing traveller, the fortunate and the unfortunate, the noble and the beggar—all pray, thank, supplicate, sigh, laud, and pour out their hearts. Fashionable ladies leave their splendid equipages and gallant attendants, and prostrate themselves in the dust with the beggars. On a holiday two or three hundred passing pilgrims may be seen kneeling before 'the Iberian Mother.' Since Alexis Michaelovitch, in 1650, the Czars have never failed to visit it frequently:

the present Emperor (meaning Alexander Paulovitsch) never omits to do so when he comes to Moscow; and it is said that he has more than once in the middle of the night wakened up the monks in order that he might perform his devotions."

It is said that this picture came from Georgia, and was carried thence to a monastery on Mount Athos, and that, some centuries after its reputation for miraculous powers had become known, it made such a stir in Russia that the Czar Alexis Michaelovitsch succeeded in getting hold of it, and established it in its present home.

Vincent Brooks, lith.

RUSSIAN NURSE.

CHAPTER VIII.

MOSCOW CONTINUED—PUBLIC BUILDINGS—RAILROAD TO NIJNI NOVGOROD — NIJNI NOVGOROD—ITS ANNUAL FAIR.

SUPERSTITIOUS ideas do not appear to be in Russia wholly confined to the lower and more uneducated classes. Those who are by many degrees above them appear to indulge in such ideas to almost the same extent. The refusal of the holy image to pay a visit to the Emperor was believed to be but one of the many signs and tokens heralding his Majesty's death.

In the great bell-tower of Ivan Velike

one of the largest bells fell on the 2nd of March, 1855, bursting through all intervening obstacles, and causing the death of some of the people who lived on the basement of the tower.

This occurrence—likely enough in itself, from the great weight of the bell—was immediately laid hold of by the superstitious minds of the people, high and low, as the forerunner of some tremendous event, and accordingly, when it was announced in Moscow on the following day that the Emperor Nicholas had died at St. Petersburg the day preceding, the wiseacres shook their heads and crossed themselves with a sort of I-told-you-so nod.

I only mention these facts as they were related to me, not with the slightest intention of turning into ridicule the religious prejudices of the people, but simply with the view of describing their ideas and feelings. Railways, education, and the progressive enlightenment of the age in which we live, will make themselves felt all in good time. There are other countries, it must be remembered, besides Russia, in which the schoolmaster, even at this day, is very much *abroad*, and out of his reckoning.

Moscow is the depôt of large quantities of every kind of merchandise, and possesses some of the most important manufactories in the whole empire. It may be said to be the centre of the internal commerce of the country. Its productions include silks, woollen cloths, manufactures of cotton, paper, carpets, and jewellery. It has, in fact, an enormous trade, which is facilitated by the railways to St. Petersburg on the one side, and Nijni Novgorod on the other. It has also, by means of the rivers and canals, a communication by water with many of the distant ports and cities.

About four miles out of Moscow is the palace built by Peter the Great, called the Petroffska Palace. On his way to this palace the tourist passes under the St. Petersburg Gate, allowed by all to be the finest of the many gates of Moscow. It is at the north-west angle of the city, and has three arches. The middle one covers the carriage-road, which is unusually wide, and the two side arches surmount the footways. On the top of the centre arch is an enormous female figure, intended to represent Victory, holding what appeared to me to be a spear in one hand and a wreath in the other, standing bolt upright in a sort of Roman car drawn by eight prancing steeds, all harnessed abreast. Seeing that Victory had no reins by which to guide her horses, one was inclined to wonder how her ladyship had managed to be so successful in her battles; but then came the reflection that a delineation of the heroic need not accord with common sense.

The panels of the arch are ornamented with imperial eagles, and, with the pillars that support its summit, are painted green, to represent malachite, I believe; the result of which is to spoil the whole appearance of the structure, and give it a tawdry and patchwork look.

The palace is, externally, an elegant building, notwithstanding its red turrets and green cupolas. The gardens are very pleasant, and when we visited them were fully occupied by the good people from the city, enjoying their tea and turn-out. It was to this palace that Napoleon betook himself when he found that its inhabitants had made Moscow too hot to hold him, and it was from here that he issued his proclamation announcing to the French people the burning of Moscow. He did not, however, remain here very long, for as the Kremlin had to a great extent escaped the ravages of the fire, he returned to the palace within its walls, where, unfortunately for himself and his army, he remained until the winter set in, which was to complete what the battle of the Borodino had commenced. It is a singular fact that in the Kremlin Palace there is but one bust, as far as I could see, and that is the bust of Napoleon, the man who was execrated by the Russians in general, and by the Moskovians in particular.

The convents in and about Moscow are numerous, and some of them cover an immense space of ground. The convent of the Donskoi, for instance, in the western suburb, is very large. It is surrounded by high walls, painted red, white, and yellow, and has battlements very much like those of the Kremlin. Inside the walls are not less than half a dozen churches or chapels, with numerous buildings for the monks, cloisters, courts, gardens, and massive towers, giving the whole affair to the outside spectator an appearance more military than ecclesiastical.

Although the Russians are open to unfavourable remarks on their superstitious notions and practices, there can be no doubt that on the score of their public benevolence, and solicitude for the welfare of the poor, they set a very good example.

There are a great many edifices for benevolent purposes around and in the city. The Foundling Hospital is an enormous establishment, though I think its name is hardly applicable in the sense in which it is used in England and in some parts of Italy. There is at Florence one of these institutions, with a mechanical contrivance to take in the deserted child, and at the same time give the mother an opportunity of escaping unseen. But at Moscow, when the child is admitted, its name and date of admission are recorded in a book, a ticket is then attached to the child's neck, and the mother receives a duplicate, upon production of which she may get the child back. The word foundling seems, therefore, misapplied.

This hospital was founded about a hundred years ago, and consists of a square building five stories high, including the basement, and forms a conspicuous object from whichever point the spectator may be looking. It has a very simple elevation, and no money has been wasted in turrets, and towers, and architectural gimcracks. The top floor is wisely appropriated to the squallers—that is, the infants in arms—whilst the elder children inhabit the floor underneath. I was told that there were not less than thirty thousand children of different ages in the establishment, which is chiefly supported by a tax on the theatres and other places of public amusement, and by a small grant from the Moscow, not from the Imperial, Government. A gift of money is sometimes left with the child, but in the case of the boys with whom no gift is made they are brought up for the army.

When any of the children evince signs of superior talent, they are educated with extra care—for engineers, governesses, &c. Many of the boys are, upon leaving the hospital, sent to the university; whilst such of the girls as are brought up to manual labour are entitled, on being married, to receive a moiety of the proceeds of their industry, the other moiety being taken towards defraying the expense of their keep in the institution.

The Galitzin Hospital, which was founded by a Prince of that name in about 1780, is a very fine building. So is Sheremetoff's Hospital, looking more like a Grecian temple than an institute for invalids. Then there are the Alexander Hospital and several others scattered in and around the city.

Moscow should be visited by all those who enjoy the novelty of viewing at a city so unlike any other in Europe, and in which the national customs and the original character of the inhabitants have undergone so little change for such a series of years. I believe that eight weeks would enable a tourist of common activity to see St. Petersburg, Moscow, and Nijni, with their suburbs and all they contain. Of course I am not allowing for any loitering on the road, but am calculating that from England the first resting-place would be Berlin, and that the traveller proceeds from that city direct to St. Petersburg. The time taken for that part of the journey is under forty-eight hours, but the carriages are so easy and comfortable that there is hardly any fatigue in performing it; whilst the expenses from England to St. Petersburg, travelling first class, do not exceed ten pounds.

Leaving Moscow with great regret, we proceeded by railroad to Nijni Novgorod, to take a look at its great annual fair.

The journey is performed at present in eighteen hours, and some part of the road, especially over one of the bridges, is rather shaky. The road had been used for some time as far as Vladimir—celebrated amongst other things for its cherry orchards—about four hours distant from Moscow, and had been opened, in consequence of the fair, earlier, perhaps, than it might otherwise have been. Next year the journey will no doubt be made in thirteen or fourteen hours, and with more comfort to the traveller.

On entering the station at Nijni, we found the inevitable ecclesiastic in his high cap soliciting alms for his church; he does not, however, bore people by much pertinacity; a simple bow sends him off to some one else.

We had received a telegram at Moscow telling us to call, on our arrival at Nijni, on his Excellency the civil governor. We found him at his bureau in full uniform, surrounded by officials. He was very kind and polite, and informed us that he had secured apartments at the Hôtel de Russie in the Old Town. His Excellency was, however, evidently puzzled to know what could have taken us to Nijni; he explained that the trade there was carried on wholesale, and asked what we wanted to buy. Upon our explaining that we were neither more nor less than tourists in search of novelty and information, and intended going to Kazan on the same errand, he exhibited surprise, and I am sure would have doubted our story had he not received letters from his friends requesting him to afford us such attentions as were within his power. After expressing his regret that he could not show us any hospitality by reason of his being so fully occupied at the close of the fair, and which we saw was really the case, he desired his servant to accompany us to the hotel and introduce us to our apartments.

These consisted of two middle-sized single-bedded rooms, without washing apparatus, for which we were to pay one guinea a day, and tenpence for the use of the sheets—these latter, in that part of the world, being considered a superfluous luxury. Although the charge for rooms appeared high, we had to take into account that it was fair time; and I believe we should have had to pay considerably more, as foreigners, had not the governor taken the rooms for us.

As to the washing apparatus, we very soon had that put right, and basins, jugs, and towels were produced by degrees, one after the other. It is wiser in these cases not to disturb or overbalance the attendant's mind or nerves by asking for everything at once. We had found out that the custom amongst the mass is to wash at a small spout, the Russians, for some reason, preferring running water for their ablutions. This spout is "open to all, and influenced by none." Excepting amongst the higher classes, it may be safely doubted whether washing is a very favourite recreation. As a Russian friend said, it saves a deal of trouble not to bother yourself about washing on a journey, and you soon get used to the want of it. At the time I thought he was joking, but after observation changed my opinion.

In a light work called "Saphir," Alexandre Dumas gives a description of the day's toilette of a Parisian exquisite. This, it appears, is conducted by his valet Jean, or Zan, as his master affectedly calls him. Whilst Zan arranges his master's hair, looks out his shirt, and puts on his Cashmere robe-de-chambre lined with satin, the dandy pares his nails, brushes his rings, polishes his eye-glass, winds up his watch, dresses himself and lights his Manilla, and is then ready *pour le combat du jour*. At night, when he goes to bed, but not before, Zan puts his master through his washing for the next day.

If the Parisian exquisite can dispense

with his morning ablutions, why not a Russian bourgeois?

At Nijni we had been told to order a soup made of the fish called "sterlet," which is certainly excellent, and is said to be the most prized of fish soups. The fish itself is very rich and oily, with a yellow-looking flesh, but exceedingly delicate withal. It is found only in the river Volga, and in winter is sent frozen to Petersburg and other places. It is, however, sent to Petersburg in the summer, though, I believe, at a very great expense; for as it must be forwarded alive, and is sent over four hundred miles in tanks filled with water from the Volga, it may be imagined that the cost is no trifle. We subsequently met with this fish at the table of an American friend of ours not far from St. Petersburg, who is well known there and in England for his liberal hospitality. On that occasion, however, the sterlet was boiled, and for the last quarter of an hour of that operation, in champagne, and served up without any other sauce, which we thought far better than when made into soup. At Nijni, too, the sturgeon is plentiful, and it is from this fish that the caviar is procured and sent all over Russia. We get it in England, but it is usually too salt. The Russians eat this caviar before sitting down to the dinner-table, whilst in England we eat it after the puddings and sweets, which they say is a piece of stupidity. There were also great numbers of very fine water-melons, which cost about tenpence apiece. These came, we were told, from Kazan. In fact, an epicure might get on very contentedly at Nijni, especially at the fair-time.

The fair, or rather bazaar, is held in

the New Town. There are long ranges and blocks of uniform one-storied wooden houses, roofed with iron, as a guard against fire.

Excepting where the knick-knacks are sold, it may be doubted whether there is much in the fair itself to amuse the mere tourist. The trader, of course, has an interest in all those countless bales and packages.

The town of Nijni Novgorod is the capital of the Government of that name, and is situated on the Volga and Oka rivers, which run through and divide what may be called the Old and New Towns. The Old Town is built on a hill, and the Kremlin, or fortification, is surrounded by a wall with round and square towers. The streets are wide, and most of them terminate in an open space on one side of the Kremlin wall. In this space is the Post-office, and here we saw in the evening large numbers of carriages waiting to carry the letters to the surrounding districts.

Inside the fortification walls is a beautiful terrace, from which the traveller obtains a most extensive view—cathedrals, an obelisk of granite, fifty feet high, to the honour of the Moscow heroes Pojarski and Minnin, and also the palaces of the governors. We drove to this place, on our arrival, in search of the governor, and when we got there found that during the fair he was obliged to reside in the New Town, so we had to wend our way back again through clouds of dust, under a burning sun, and in one of those horrid droschkies, which, after eighteen hours in a railway carriage, was a trial of the temper. Of all the uncomfortable carriages which it has ever been my lot to travel in (and I thought that wretched six inside affair over the desert between Suez and Cairo was bad enough), I think the droschky beats them all. Of course I speak of those that do duty for hack carriages.

In one class of this carriage the traveller sits astride upon a narrow ledge in the middle, close behind the driver, who, in most instances, gives out an odour not at all like lavender-water, nor anything else that is pleasant to the nostrils; whilst in another class there is a hard leather seat, which, by continual use, has obtained a shiny slippery surface, upon which I defy any one but a Russian to remain two minutes, unless he holds on like grim death to the little iron bar which runs along on a level with the seat, but otherwise is not of the slightest service in keeping a man on it. In that abominable cruise up and down Nijni that day, my wife and the crinoline and I had to manage to keep ourselves steady on one of the smallest and slipperiest of those slippery cushions, and what with holding an umbrella over her, and holding on at the same time to that confounded iron bar, I confess I did wish myself anywhere else.

In the middle of it, however, crack we came against another of these "infernal machines." And off went one of our traces.

It is the custom here to fasten the traces to the axletrees just outside the linchpin. And as the traces are kept pretty tight, no amount of coaxing the obdurate rope, or twisting the front wheels nearer, would do so. As in the mysterious mode of Russian harnessing the fixing the traces is the first business, our bearded, long-coated Jehu deliberately proceeded to take off all the harness until he could pay out enough of the slack of that obstinate trace to get it over the axletree again. This operation certainly cost us twenty minutes, and all that time we sat jammed up on the narrow seat, nearly stifled with dust, and frying in the sun, as hot, and almost as flat, as pancakes.

There are numerous churches—many of a large size—monasteries, nunneries, schools, and other public buildings. The view from the top of the hill over the Volga, stretching away towards Tartary, was the most extensive we had seen in Russia. Steamers of all sizes were lying on this portion of the river, ready to start on their voyage to Kazan, whilst a great number of smaller ones were plying between the shores. Lower down was a steam-engine manufactory, worked by an Englishman.

The fair was, two or three hundred years

ago, held at Kazan, which is thirty-six hours' steaming up the Volga; but about that time it was removed from there to some place, of which I could not, however, retain the name, nearer to Nijni Novgorod. It was not, however, much more than forty years ago that it was brought to its present site. The fair commences at the end of June, and lasts for two months. The resident population of Nijni is about twenty-four thousand; but during the fair this number is increased to close upon four hundred thousand, made up of people from all parts of Russia, and other countries. I was told that the fair this year was the largest ever known, and that the value of the goods taken there for sale could not have been much under nine millions sterling. Perhaps this estimate was exaggerated; indeed, it is difficult to see how any one, not having access to official documents, could form an estimate at all. The quantities of goods, however, piled up near the railway station, were enough to take away one's breath, whilst the long lines of carts, filled with different kinds of merchandise, which we met with in our drives in the country, were unaccountable. We were told by the governor that nearly all the goods and merchandise had been sold.

These goods and merchandise appear to comprise everything that was ever made or heard of. There was tea from China, and Russian wine and brandy; there were turquoises from Bokhara, and Russian train-oil and caviar; there was wool from Cashmere and Russian hempen textures; carpets and raw silk from Persia, and silks and cottons from China; refined sugar from Archangel, and soap from Kazan; there were horses' hides and dried fish, porcelain and washed rags, glass and mirrors, paper, horses' tails, furs, worked skins, and copper goods, coffee and cochineal, feathers and drugs, hogs' bristles, tobacco, ceintures and slippers, of which two latter we became purchasers to a small extent: in fact, there was nothing one could not buy, from a handspike to a handkerchief.

The ceintures were worked in gold and silver thread, and were very much like those we had previously seen in the Great Exhibition at Brompton, and to which some pretty young ladies of our acquaintance had taken a fancy, but which they were too late to obtain for love or money, and so, by way of doing the amiable, we ministered to their wants at Nijni instead of at Brompton. We also bought a small quantity of the Kazan soap, one species of which, called "the rose," cost a little over twenty shillings the English pound-weight. One did thank one's stars that that article was scarce in England; and it was pardonable to think that if all soap in Russia cost that money, it was some excuse for the people not using much of it.

We "did," as it is called, the fair thoroughly, and one of us was extremely glad when that desideratum had been finally obtained, and he was enabled to rest from his labours. The clouds of dust and the heat of the sun were a drawback on personal comfort, and, as before said, there is not much in the fair to interest the general tourist. To those, however, who are amused by the gregarious assembling of Jews, Turks, infidels and heretics, the scene presented at the New Town entrance to the bridge of boats which divides the two towns would afford great attractions. The traffic and crowd at this spot are beyond description. London-bridge is thronged in its overflow by carriages, cabs, and carts; the bridge at Nijni is thronged by human beings, vehicles being rather the exception. Order is preserved by foot and mounted Cossack soldiers, whose chief arm is a whip. We did not see it administered, but it was held apparently quite ready for any emergency. The mob, for it could be called by no other name, was very dense, and comprised people of all sorts, sizes, colours, and costumes. The round English hat, the Armenian high-peaked cap, the turban, and the labourer's hat, which could only be likened to Paddy's from Cork without a rim, were all jumbled up together in the most ludicrous confusion; but I do not think I saw one solitary specimen of the fair sex amongst all that crowd; notwithstanding which, there was no end of chattering, and some small amount of squabbling.

The province of Nijni Novgorod is said to be one of the best cultivated, and at the same time most fertile, of all the provinces of Imperial Russia. The people grow large quantities of flax and hemp, also rye, hops, and the common vegetables and fruits. The forests are of enormous extent, and contain oak, lime, pine and beech trees. The Government, as well as many private persons, have establishments for breeding horses, and it is asserted that the best Russian-bred horses come from this province. The climate is comparatively mild; there is not much moisture, and the spring and autumn are more equable than in Moscow. Longevity is very noticeable, and in some years the number of births nearly doubles the number of deaths.

In the country districts of the province there are large establishments for the manufacture of woollen cloth, soap, iron, leather, linen, &c., and in the town the inhabitants manufacture lace of a coarse kind, cordage, copper, and iron articles, &c.

On a space of ground enclosed by a broad canal in the shape of a horse-shoe, and which, for the sake of distinction, I used to call the New Town, is almost a city of magazines, built in the shape of an oblong parallelogram, surrounded by shops. In this locale is a spacious building, in which the local authorities take up their residence during the fair, and it is here that the fair is held.

Extending behind this parallelogram are blocks of buildings, intersected by streets running at right angles with one another. The number of the shops is about three thousand. A good broad street goes through the centre of this mass of buildings, and is terminated by a very handsome church, whilst at one end of the fair is a handsome mosque for the Mahometans. The Chinese shops are built in a very fantastic manner, and sport lots of gay flags and streamers, which give a holiday air to the scene. There is a very good theatre, and a fair sprinkling of Tartar restaurants. On both sides of the bridge of boats, and extending I don't know how far, there is a mass of lighters, barges, and vessels, which I should think must have been made after the model of Noah's ark, so inconceivably ugly and clumsy are they. It is said that there are upwards of fifty thousand people, from the borders of Europe and Asia, who are employed in navigating them. The river Oka at this point must be broader than our dear dirty old Thames at London-bridge.

Whilst strolling up and down the streets of the Old Town, I came upon several gangs of convicts returning from their day's work. They were all coarsely and uniformly clothed, and were marching in files two abreast. Each gang contained about thirty men, and were guarded by two or three armed soldiers. One or two of the convicts addressed some observations to us, and I concluded by their holding out their hands that they were asking for money. The soldiers did not interfere with them, but as I did not know what might happen if I gave them anything, I took the safer course of keeping myself to myself.

I had seen several of these gangs at work on the banks of the river at Wilna, and had been told that they were men who had been convicted of petty thefts and crimes.

Those who are guilty of higher offences, and receive sentences for long terms of years or for life, are sent off to Siberia to work in the mines, or in the Government manufactories. When they have worked out their sentences, or for good behaviour have received a commutation of them, they get tickets of leave, and are dispersed over the villages in Siberia, or have land granted to them by the Government at an annual rental, but neither they nor their children are allowed to leave the place where they are so established. It does seem very hard that the sins of the father should be thus visited on the children —but so it is.

It is supposed by many persons in England that political prisoners, when sent to Siberia, are condemned to the public works.

Vincent Brooks, lith

SHOPWOMAN IN HOLIDAY DRESS.

What the system might have been years ago I don't know, but at the present day that is not the case. Political prisoners are exiled to some place in Siberia, and are free to pass their time as they like, but are prohibited from leaving it. Escapes from Siberia, I believe, are rare enough, and there must be great difficulties in getting out of a country where the inhabitants are constantly asked for their passports in moving about.

Talking of passports reminds me of a conversation I had with a Russian lady, who was pitying me for living in England, where, as she said, everything down to tea and sugar was taxed, whilst in Russia all was comparatively free from duty. On asking her how the army and police were kept up and paid, she naïvely remarked that the Emperor took all that on himself; and on my replying that his Majesty must be very rich, she said, "Oh, but you know he receives a great deal for our passports;" and then I learned that every person in Russia, from the highest to the lowest, foreigner as well as native, pays every year so much for his passport, the scales of payment being adapted to the different classes of the people; so that where a noble of large means may pay 50*l.*, the peasant pays only a few shillings. I suggested to my fair friend that that system appeared to me something like our income-tax, against which she had just previously inveighed so eloquently but femininely; but it was of no use; she would not have it, and could not see it, so I allowed her to go on pitying the poor English, which I have no doubt she continues to do to this day.

As the authorities at Nijni were very particular about the passports of strangers being strictly *en règle*, caused, as I was informed, by the numerous incendiarisms in Petersburg and elsewhere, and which I heard had been threatened in Nijni, I walked down to the police-office to get my passport put straight.

Passing through several rooms, I arrived at last at one in which the chief of the police was engaged in trying a person for passing bad money, and whom I recognised as a passenger in the same train as that by which I had arrived the previous day.

At the head of the table sat the chief of the police in his uniform, and at the bottom of it was a large square box with the Russian eagle surmounting it. This box, I was told, was intended to represent or typify "The Law." It was evidently the wrong box for the prisoner, for he was, in a very few minutes, found guilty, and sent off to prison for a couple of years.

After he had been disposed of, I made my way into the room, and was passed along to the passport clerk, who was surrounded by numbers of people on the same errand. My English costume immediately attracted the clerk's notice, and I was beckoned forwards, the Armenians and others making way for me in the most polite manner. After answering all sorts of funny questions as to age, country, calling, and some domestic inquiries as to wife, and I think children, my friend came to the question of my religion. I answered, "Protestant," which bothered him immensely, and excited the least possible shrug of the shoulders from some of the bystanders. After a little time, however, the clerk said something in Russian which was much approved of by those around, and which, I believe, conveyed that he had never heard of such a religion as that, and that he supposed I had none at all. However, I obtained the necessary visé to my passport, made my salaam, and walked off.

CHAPTER IX.

DEPARTURE FROM NIJNI NOVGOROD—ARRIVAL AT ST. PETERSBURG—THE WINTER PALACE —THE HERMITAGE—THE CHURCH OF ST. ISAAC.

WE had intended to continue our journey to Kazan, but found that our time would not allow of it. It is a very old Tartar town, and is easy enough of access from Nijni by steamers, which perform the journey in thirty-eight or forty hours. It was represented to us as not containing many attractions for the tourist; and as the fair was approaching its end, the steam-boats were crowded with the vendors returning to their homes, a close companionship with some of whom for the best part of two days was not likely to conduce to pleasure or comfort; so, after a few days' stay in Nijni, and thirty-eight hours on the railroad, we found ourselves at eight o'clock one morning in St. Petersburg driving to Zähringer's Hotel in the Admiralty-square, and which, for the information of fellow-travellers, I may here say we found very comfortable, with reasonable charges. We had two large rooms on the second floor looking on the Place de l'Amirauté. They were fitted up, one as a dining-room and the other as a drawing-room, with screens, behind which were beds. For these we paid fourteen shillings a day. The house was clean and the cuisine good, without being too expensive.

As we drove down the splendid street called Nevskoi Perspective, nearly two miles in length, we saw by the mounted gendarmes in their light-blue uniforms, stationed at close intervals, that a fête was on the tapis.

On inquiry, we were told that the Emperor was to take part in a grand procession to the Alexander Nevskoi church and monastery. We turned out to see what was going on, and were just in time to catch the end of it, but, owing to the great crowd, were unable to obtain more than a glimpse of the Emperor. There was the usual long line of priests, who, as they passed where we were standing, came to a halt, and chanted a hymn in front of one of the Emperor's palaces. The Empress had just entered, and the crowd were cheering her. There were the state carriages, nine in number, drawn some by eight and others by six horses, reminding one of a similar scene when her Majesty opens the parliamentary session in London.

Of course we paid a visit to the Winter Palace, to enter which the gentlemen are obliged to put on their dress-coats, which is an absurd nuisance. The palace was undergoing repairs and decorations. The old palace, built in the middle of the last century, was destroyed by fire in 1837, and the present one is reputed by the Russians themselves to be the most magnificent and extensive royal palace in existence. It is situated on the Neva, which is here, and for a considerable space beyond, embanked by a wall and parapet of granite, which sparkles brightly in the sunlight. The front of the palace extends upwards of seven hundred English feet, is almost square, and is three stories high. We were shown a corner room looking on the river, which his present Majesty uses as his own particular one, and where he transacts his daily work. When the imperial family are residing here, it is said that upwards of six thousand people are quartered in the building. The room, or rather hall, in which the Empress receives her guests, has its walls almost covered with gold; but St. George's Hall, in which there is a magnificent throne, is the chief apartment. It is one hundred and fifty feet long by sixty feet wide, and, although not appearing to advantage, in consequence of the numbers of workmen engaged in the redecorations, is one of the most splendid and noble apartments we had ever seen, and it is in this that the Emperor receives the foreign ambassadors. Near this hall is a picture-gallery of the Generals who served during the invasion of 1812 and the subsequent battles, and beyond it is the Field-Marshals' gallery, in which "our Duke" has a permanent place.

In a part of the palace, away from these grand public rooms, we were shown into a small apartment which the late Emperor used as his bedroom, and in which he died. The furniture was simple enough, with a small camp bed without curtains, at the head of which, on the wall, was a picture of a favourite daughter, whilst on his writing and toilet tables everything, down to his pocket-handkerchief, was left as he had used them just before his death.

A secret staircase communicated with the Empress's room below, which was fitted up and furnished—as ladies' rooms should be—very handsomely.

On the side of the palace, forming part of the Admiralty-square, was a huge cylinder, partly sunk in the ground, constructed for an open-air fire in the winter for the benefit of the coachmen and servants whilst waiting at night for their masters. Certainly a necessary precaution in a climate where the frost is so intense as to have cracked the solid granite column erected close by to the honour and memory of Alexander the First. The Hermitage, adjoining the Winter Palace, contains acres of pictures—Vandykes, Raphaels, Corregios, Murillos, and, in fact, all the celebrated masters. It would take weeks to see thoroughly, and a volume to describe, the treasures and curiosities collected here.

From one of the treasure-rooms in this building, notwithstanding the attendant's presence, was stolen, some few years ago, a very valuable ring. This, as we were informed, was sold by the thief to a jeweller, who sold it again to some one who made it a present to one of the members of the imperial family. It was immediately recognised, inquiries set on foot, and the thief discovered. As he was of considerable standing and position, the matter was, as is not unusual in Russia, hushed up, and but few people know his name.

The room containing the crowns, precious stones, and jewels of the imperial family, should on no account be passed by without a visit. The Emperor's crown is ornamented with oak-leaves formed of the largest and purest diamonds, whilst the imperial sceptre is resplendent with one diamond, which is said to be the largest in the world, and to have been bought by Catherine the Second. On either side of the door admitting to this room are armed sentries, and, calling to mind the daring attempt of Colonel Blood and his friend Mr. Parrett in 1671 to walk off with the crown of England and the paraphernalia—in which, by the way, the two scamps were nearly successful—one need not be surprised that in Russia such precautions as armed sentries are resorted to even in 1862.

The "Hermitage" was erected by Catherine II. It escaped the great fire in 1837, being saved by the exertions of the military and Mujiks.

This building is connected with the Winter Palace by covered galleries, and may be said to be a continuation of the palace itself.

The collection of paintings occupies at least forty rooms, and must be of enormous value. The ground floor is filled with statuary, some being very choice specimens. In this building is also a library, consisting of more than fifteen thousand volumes in the Russian language. This library was formed by Catherine for the instruction of her numerous attendants, and in it are also the collections of Voltaire and other remarkable men, comprising, altogether, upwards of one hundred and fifty thousand volumes.

In one of the rooms is a magnificent vase of lilac jasper from Siberia, standing five feet high, of an elegant design, and very highly polished. There are also tripods, which are said to be of solid gold, seven feet high, supporting golden salvers, on which bread and salt were handed to the Emperor Alexander on his return from Paris in 1815. There is also a very curious clock, called the Peacock's Clock, which the attendant informed us was of English manufacture, which I doubt, and which was presented by Prince Potemkin to his royal mistress and sovereign. It is enclosed in a glass case, ten or twelve feet high: the form of the clock is that of a tree, the branches and leaves being of gold; a peacock sits on the top of the tree, and playfully expands his gaudy tail when the chimes ring; but as the machinery is out of order, and the chimes never do ring, the peacock gets a rest, as does also the gold cock, whose duty it is to flap his wings and crow to mark the hours.

In the lower rooms may be seen more of the working tools of Peter the Great, with numerous articles of his own manufacture, such as bars of iron wrought by his hand, models of ships, and samples of rope. In fact, his Majesty must have been a regular Jack-of-all-trades; but I confess that he appears to have differed from the generality of that class, in so far as he seems to have been a tolerable master of many of them.

We visited the church of St. Peter and St. Paul in the fortress, where are the tombs of Peter the Great and of all the sovereigns, and many of their families, since that period. The church is well stored with flags and banners taken in battles. The old militaire in charge pointed with a knowing smile to a bundle of these discoloured flags, as old as the hills, nailed up on one of the columns, and said they had been captured from the English. The Russians are brave enough, no doubt, to take the flags of any people when the fortune of war favours them, but they never did take any of ours until they got hold of the *Tiger's* in the late war, when that vessel went ashore. I asked my old friend when and where those that he pointed out were captured. I suppose my manner was rather sharp with him, for he put on a grave face, and admitted his ignorance. A few extra copecks at parting, however, restored the entente cordiale between us.

The visitor to St. Petersburg should on no account omit two or three visits to the magnificent Isaac's Church. In one of the chapels are two large columns of lapis-lazuli, said by some, but denied by others, to be each of one solid piece, whilst of malachite there are nearly a dozen.

The Russian churches, both at Moscow and St. Petersburg, contain solid silver ornaments, and the images are covered with precious stones of enormous value;

but Isaac's Church exceeds them all in the costly magnificence of its contents.

The foundation of this church was laid by Catherine II. about one hundred and ten years ago. The late Emperor Nicholas completed it. Its foundation, I was told, cost more than 230,000*l.* of English money. I believe no one knows what this church did actually cost.

I once heard of a nobleman in England who built a splendid palace, and who, when the day of reckoning came, and the bills of the architects and builders were delivered, was so disgusted at their amount, that, after paying them, he tossed them into the fire, so that his heir should never know the extent of his ancestor's folly or extravagance.

Such, I rather think, must be the case with the Church of St. Isaac. I don't believe that any one knows what sums have been laid out upon it, but I was told in St.

Petersburg that moneys equal to 18,000,000*l.* English have been expended on it.

It is built in the form of a Greek cross, having its four sides equal in size. At the entrance are polished monolithic pillars of Finland granite, sixty-four feet high, with a diameter of seven feet. The steps by which it is approached are very grand, and of the same material. The cupola is roofed with copper, covered with burnished gold, which, reflecting the rays of the sun, is a conspicuous and magnificent object for miles before the city is reached. Above this cupola is an immense gilt cross. This church, however, is not so large as our St. Paul's Cathedral, nor even as the cathedral at Milan, which is 443 English feet within the walls.

Architectural critics affirm that to give complete effect to the building it should have had a greater elevation than it possesses by some seven or eight feet.

Incredible as it may appear to the uninstructed in these matters, we were informed that, not very long ago, it was in contemplation to raise this enormous building some feet, foundations and all; that plans were actually made for the purpose; and that nothing but the enormous expense of the work prevented its being carried out.

Imagine the idea of raising our St. Paul's bodily eight feet above its present position! In England it would be almost unsafe for an architect to propound such a scheme—he would in all probability be looked upon as a madman; but there are people in this country who have seen the plans, and who can testify to the truth of what I have stated.

CHAPTER X.

ST. PETERSBURG CONTINUED — THE KAZAN CHURCH—HUT OF PETER THE GREAT—THE OPERA HOUSE—JAPANESE AMBASSADORS—SMOKING—PETERHOF—GENERAL DESCRIPTION.

THE metropolitan church in the Nevskoi Perspective, dedicated to the Lady of Kazan, has a colonnade of Corinthian columns, stretching from the church towards the street. This colonnade looks like an attempt to copy that of St. Peter's at Rome, but, if it be so, it is an obvious failure. The Russian one is not high enough, nor long enough, and it breaks off at each end in such an abrupt termination, that the spectator is induced to ask whether it was originally intended to remain in its present condition.

In front of the cathedral are two statues, one of Barclay de Tolly, the other of Kutusoff, who went here to pray before the picture of the Mother of God of Kazan, prior to his leaving, in 1812, for Moscow. This picture was originally in the Tartar church at Kazan, but was brought from there by Ivan Wassilievitsch, who seems to have been a great hand at that sort of thing, and deposited at Moscow, until Peter the Great had it removed to St. Petersburg. The interior of the church is filled with upwards of fifty immense monolithic columns, which, although peculiarly imposing, are somewhat gloomy, and are clearly not wanted to support the roof.

There is a profusion of silver ornamentation in the interior, which is due to the pious exertions of the Cossacks, who laid their booty in 1813 as an offering at the shrine of the Mother of Kazan.

The church and convent dedicated to St. Alexander Nevskoi, he who defeated the Swedes on the Neva, are situated at the end of the Nevskoi Perspective, and are well worthy of a visit. They were founded by Peter the Great, and were originally built of wood, but were subsequently replaced by the present stone edifices. The monument to Alexander Nevskoi is in one of the side-chapels, and is said to be made of solid silver: it is in the form of a pyramid, fifteen feet high. The Roman Catholic, the Armenian, and other churches, scattered about all parts of the city, attest the religious tolerance of the Russian Government. When we were in Rome, in 1857, we found that a Protestant church was not allowed within its walls. But Rome is by some people considered as a highly civilised spot, whilst Russia is looked upon by them as a semi-barbarous country.

Opposite the Isaac's Church is a monument to the late Emperor Nicholas. His Majesty is represented on horseback, in the full uniform of one of his favourite regiments, with a dove or a pigeon on his helmet. The pigeon is held sacred in Russia, and is not eaten by the devout. The likeness to the Emperor is stated to be exact. This monument must have cost a large sum of money, but does not contrast favourably with the noble simplicity of that of Peter the Great, bareheaded, with his horse's hind legs trampling on a serpent, the whole standing on one immense solid block of granite.

Turning, however, from the colossal buildings which ornament St. Petersburg, we went in search of the little hut by the river's side built and inhabited by Peter the Great when he first went to lay the foundations of that city. We had some difficulty in finding it, for our coachman, although he had never been out of St. Petersburg, and the courier, whose duty it was to know everything of the kind, had never heard of it. Such is fame!

At last, after many inquiries, we reached it, and found it to consist of two rooms, one of which is converted into a chapel; the other contained some of the working tools and numerous souvenirs of the Emperor; amongst others, a six-oared boat, the work of his own hands, and far better made than those ugly boats at the Moscow palace. The old hut is now surrounded by walls, and roofed over to preserve it from the weather. It is an interesting memento, not only as being the humble dwelling of Peter the

Great, but as the first house built in St. Petersburg.

The Opera House is a fine building, and well arranged inside for hearing and seeing. It is, like all similar establishments, under the immediate management and control of the Government, by whom the whole expense is defrayed, and servants in the imperial livery usher you to your seats. Here, in two boxes opposite, were their high mightinesses the Japanese ambassadors and suite. They appeared very merry, as well they might be, seeing that they have been living like fighting-cocks for the last month at the expense of the Government. They left the following day, and about a month afterwards we found them again at the Grand Hotel in Paris. There was a story afloat that they had told the people at Berlin that they liked them better than the

English or French, as they more resembled themselves in their tastes and habits. If this story were true, the Berliners would hardly accept the intended compliment with pleasure. I suspect, however, that it was a malicious joke of the wags at St. Petersburg.

The Imperial loge is in the centre. There is a smoking-room, but it is not ventilated in the least degree. When I went into it, it was impossible to see a hand's breadth before you, so dense was the smoke. No one is allowed to smoke in the streets of St. Petersburg, so the gentlemen take every opportunity of indulging in cigars in every other place. Certainly the practice is not pleasant, shut up all night in a railway carriage. As a matter of theory, it is said that smoking is not allowed in first-class carriages, but, as a matter of practice, the case is reversed. Travelling up from Nijni Novgorod to Moscow, one of the passengers put the question whether any one objected to smoking. As the carriage was full, and as I felt perfectly certain, from the "cut of their jibs," that four out of five of the other passengers would smoke, if they smoked at all, tobacco of the worst description, I resolved, at the risk of making myself hated for ever, to say that I objected to it. We had been for an hour and a half previously nearly suffocated with smoke and the most villanous odours of all kinds in the waiting-room of the station. Upon my objecting to undergoing the same process in the railway carriage, I was met by the observation that foreigners (there it might mean any one but Russians or Poles) always objected to everything. I stood my ground, however, simply saying that it was easy to call the conductor, and that if he said smoking was permitted, we must bend to the custom; but that, if not, they must refrain. The conductor was called, and he gave it against me. It is true that the other passengers spoke Russ and I did not, so they might have taken a dirty advantage of me. I contented myself by saying quietly that a Russian gentleman had told me no one had a right to smoke in a first-class carriage, with or without permission, and that when I got to St. Petersburg I would make further inquiries. The result was that there was no smoking, and I was not slow in divining the reason.

The best way in all these matters is to be very firm, letting people see that whilst you are ready to conform to the law, you expect them to do so likewise. I was surprised to see, whilst travelling, so many elegant young women, evidently of the higher class, availing themselves of the stoppage of the trains to get out and have a smoke. It did not look nice to see them go to work in the methodical way they set about it. Out came a great he-looking cigar-case and a light-striking machine, and in a brace of shakes those pretty lips were disfigured with a black-looking cigar, from which ascended clouds of smoke, rendering them unpleasant to approach for the rest of the day. However, as their husbands did not appear to object, I suppose no one else need do so.

But to return to St. Petersburg. No one should omit driving through the islands. These are covered with gardens, avenues of trees, palaces, and country-houses, and in the height of summer a residence in any one of them must be delightful. The roads are well kept, the shade of the trees most grateful, and the peeps every now and then down the Neva very beautiful. We were rather late in the season for the full enjoyment of these charming localities, and found it quite cold enough in the middle of September, when returning from a dinner-party at ten o'clock at night in an open carriage.

We paid a visit to Peterhof to see *les grandes eaux*, which we had heard rivalled, if they did not exceed, those at Versailles. On the whole, we thought those at Peterhof the best. The avenue of these fountains in front of the palace was in every way more picturesque and effective than anything at Versailles. The statue of Samson throwing up the water to a very great height is not equalled anywhere. Perhaps there is no one particular fountain at Peterhof to equal that of the group of Neptune at Versailles, but, as a whole, we thought that the Russian exhibition beat the French one. At Peterhof we went to dine at the Bellevue restaurant, the best in the place, but were dreadfully disgusted at finding that the cook, waiters, and all, had gone to St. Petersburg to see the illuminations which were coming off that evening in honour of the Millennium Commemoration at Novgorod Welike. We managed, however, to get a sort of dinner, with some tolerable champagne, and intolerably dirty napkins, which latter must have done service for a week in the kitchen before they were allotted to us. They very soon found themselves in a far-off corner of the room.

The charge for the dinner, however, was just as high as if the cook and waiters had all been at their posts.

That dinner brought poor Theodore Hook to my mind. He told a story about ordering a dinner somewhere down the river Thames. Upon asking the waiter what was available in the inn, he was answered, everything; but as he named one dish after another, none of which were forthcoming, he asked what actually was in the house, and received the unfortunate waiter's reply, of which Hook well knew the sad meaning, "There's an execution, sir." And so it was with us at Peterhof. According to the garçon's statement, there was everything to be had. It resulted in tsche, a very ordinary Russian soup, and some réchauffé boiled beef of the driest description.

In the evening we went to see the illuminations in St. Petersburg, and very good they were. There was an immense concourse, but no pushing or rough behaviour. We were in three or four crowds in Russia, and were obliged to admit that had we been amongst the same number of persons in another place, London, for example, we might not have fared so well.

Before leaving St. Petersburg, a short general description of it may not be unamusing to those who have not yet visited it.

It was founded in 1703, on ground which

Vincent Brooks, lith.

ICE BREAKER.

had formerly belonged to the Swedes, and was then a low marshy place, but eminently suitable as a spot from which communications could be had with Europe. Peter the Great died about twenty-two years after he had founded it, at which time St. Petersburg is said to have numbered upwards of 80,000 inhabitants, whilst the population at the present time exceeds 600,000.

The roadways are very broad, and lined on either side with churches, stately palaces, and handsome shops, at which, by the way, we found everything exceedingly dear. Good canals run through the city, whilst the quays and ramparts, and many of the public buildings, are built entirely of granite, brought from a great distance at an enormous expense.

The streets, however, although a decided improvement on the Moscow ones, are badly paved, and require to be re-laid every year in some parts of the city.

The Nevskoi Perspective for a long way is paved with wood, which is very soothing to the senses after roughing it over the jolting stones. In the winter, when the snow is on the ground, and sledges are used, the inhabitants get along smoothly enough.

I was informed that there are no wells in St. Petersburg, the people depending entirely on the Neva for their supply of water, and which they hold in great estimation. Strangers, however, are always cautioned against taking too much of it at first. I did not fall into that error first or last. And were it not for the fear of shocking the sensitive nerves of some of my total abstaining friends, I would at once admit that I found champagne and Seltzer-water a much safer, as well as a much pleasanter, beverage. Old Horace says:

——nec vivere carmina possunt,
Quæ scribuntur aquæ potoribus;

and I agree with the sentiment in more senses than the one he speaks of, although declaring myself, at the same time, a perfect devotee to the charms of Bohea.

As already stated, St. Petersburg stands on a low, swampy, marshy ground, which, with the surrounding country, is liable to be, and often is, inundated by the river Neva, which in ordinary seasons is frozen about the beginning or middle of November, and remains so until the end of March. Spring is not gradual as in England, but the summer comes in, as in Australia, with a rush, and the inhabitants, as though determined to make up for the wearisome hours in which they have been caged during the winter, swarm out like butterflies to bask in the genial sunshine.

I was told that during the summer nights

large parties crowd the streets, whilst the river is merry with boating expeditions, and the song and music float gently and harmoniously in the air. I can speak a good word for the bright and warm delicious nights of a Russian summer.

But towards the end of September we experienced cold cutting winds, finding their way into the very marrow of one's bones; making a March wind in England by comparison a pleasant affair.

St. Petersburg is one of the greatest manufacturing depôts of the empire. There they make silk, leather, woollen, glass, and gold and silver articles, snuff, but not good, as I know to my cost, watches, and sugar. There is an English company that manufactures splendid bronze monuments and statues, beautifully bound books, studded with malachite and other ornaments, and gold and silver plate of exquisite fashion and taste.

In this city the Government carries on works on its own account; such as the manufacture of plate glass, where mirrors of a very large size can be procured, aquafortis, porcelain, tapestry, cotton and linen, in the making of which latter steam-engines are employed. There is also an establishment for founding cannon, a mint, and several powder-mills.

The trade at St. Petersburg is by no means inconsiderable. Although ships of large burden cannot go to the wharves and quays of the city, in consequence of a bar across the entrance of the Neva, which ordinarily has not more than nine feet water on it, the trade is carried on by steamers and lighters, which land the merchandise and goods from the larger ships.

The exports mainly consist of hemp and flax, which are sent to St. Petersburg from the neighbouring provinces of Pskoff, Finland, and Novgorod, timber, potash, furs, iron, and copper.

The imports consist chiefly of produce from the provinces—dye-stuffs, tissues of cotton, flax, wool, silk, wine and spirits, and teas from China.

At St. Petersburg are also constructed ships which, when of a large measurement, are conducted down the river by steamers to Cronstadt, where they are fitted up, and got ready for sea.

There is a large canal connecting the Neva with the Volga, thereby giving a water-communication between the Baltic and Caspian Seas, covering a distance of something like thirteen hundred and odd miles.

CHAPTER XI.

DEPARTURE FROM ST. PETERSBURG — PASSPORTS — RAILWAY STATIONS — POLAND — CROSSING THE FRONTIER — EXCISE LAWS.

Having seen as much of St. Petersburg as we could hope to see at that season of the year, we made our arrangements for a start home, and amongst them was the necessary one as to our passports. The rule in Russia, which we did not then know, but afterwards, to our cost, found out, is that all foreigners who have been resident in Russia more than seven days must have a Russian passport to carry them across the frontier. I had taken the precaution of inquiring at the British embassy, but, oddly enough, the gentleman whom I saw there did not know much about the passport regulations. I must add, however, that he was very polite and obliging. We therefore desired the courier to do the needful for us in this matter, and although we had discovered that he was an idle, good-for-nothing fellow, thought we might trust him in so simple an affair as this. I had paid him some eight shillings for stamped paper and signatures in respect of this document, and the day before leaving asked for it. It was not then ready, was his answer, but would be all right next morning. So next morning we asked again for it, but the reply was, that in consequence of the fête on the previous day the official top-sawyer had not gone to the bureau. "Mais soyez tranquil, monsieur; I'll send it by the evening's post to you, aux soins de son excellence à Pskoff."

We were not going farther that day than Pskoff, eight hours from St. Petersburg, the governor having kindly invited us to dine and sleep at his house, and thus break the length of the journey to Berlin.

It was too late then to alter our plans, so off we started, at six o'clock in the morning, to take the rail for Pskoff; and rather lucky it was for us that we had left our beds betimes, for, on getting into the street, there were no droschkies provided, and we had to begin our journey on foot, and it was not until we had nearly arrived at the station that our *bête noire*, in the person of the courier, overtook us. The first thing that attracted our attention was my portmanteau making sundry grotesque rollings over in the street, in its descent from the back of the droschky.

Nevertheless, we arrived in good time at the station, got our baggage weighed, tickets paid for, and all ready to take our places in the carriages.

But there is the same bad rule in Russia, as in France, Germany, and some other countries, by which every traveller is locked into a waiting-room until a few minutes before the train starts.

Still, in other countries, there certainly is fair play, which there is not in Russia.

A stranger goes to the station at St. Petersburg, Moscow, or Nijni Novgorod, pays his money, but doesn't take his choice. That is reserved for those who wear the Russian uniform. These gentlemen enter the station, very often, as I have seen, in a domineering manner, walk through the crowds of people, order the attendants to open the door leading to the carriages, select the best places for themselves, deposit their pillows, blankets, and carpet-bags, and then quietly saunter back with an air of superiority far from agreeable to the lookers-on.

At the prescribed time for opening the station doors, the outside, ununiformed public are allowed to go and cater for themselves, which catering consists in securing whatever places the privileged ones have left unoccupied.

Now, upon a journey of three or four hours, this would not be a grievance worth thinking of, because a man of the world could swallow the unfairness of the thing with a grimace or two. But when the journey is to last all through the night and well into the next day, one does feel, when all pay equally, that people in plain clothes are treated unfairly by being obliged to wait in the attendance-room, whilst Russian officers in uniform, who in many cases pay nothing, are allowed to walk past the officials and secure a comfortable berth for themselves.

It is all very well to say that, when people travel, they must conform to the usages of the country in which they may happen to find themselves. No doubt foreigners should do so; but, in the instance to which I refer, it is the native who breaks the regulations of his own country at the expense of the travelling public, and, at this time of day, it is rather too much that any particular set of men should be allowed to lord it over ladies and gentlemen in the manner referred to.

At one station, I got over the difficulty after a time, by administering a little palm oil in the shape of some copecks; but that is not a good system.

On our way to Pskoff we found ourselves in a railway carriage with three gentlemen, one of whom was a Polish officer. We soon fell into conversation, and a very intelligent, good, loyal fellow he appeared to be. Amongst other things, he said that all that was wanted to send Russia ahead was a sufficient population; that the country contained within itself gold and silver, iron, copper, timber, hemp, flax, and corn, everything, in fact, that was necessary for its wealth, manufactures, luxury, support, and trade; but the want of population rendered the country too dependent on the foreigner. He spoke warmly in favour of a large united empire.

We became as great friends as a journey of eight hours was capable of making men of different ideas and languages, and, before we parted, exchanged our cartes de visite and a hearty shake of the hand. This gentleman was quartered at Wilna, the first town at which we had stopped in Russia.

Talking of Poland with several persons in

Russia, I could not escape the idea that there was a sort of uneasy feeling abroad with regard to that country.

It was stated to me by one gentleman, on whose good sense and moderate views I was inclined to place reliance, that the Emperor and the Grand-Duke Constantine had shown the Poles more kindness, and invested them with twice the number of rights and privileges, that the subjects of Russia proper possessed. Of course I don't endorse this statement, for I had no means of testing its truth. But I thought I detected an under stratum of opinion that, could the question of boundaries be satisfactorily defined, the Russian Government might be rather glad than otherwise to come to some arrangement by which a kingdom of Poland might be reconstituted, but that a difficulty existed in this direction in consequence of the Poles claiming to incorporate in their kingdom some seven or eight provinces which, during their continual skrimmages with Russia, they had at some time or other conquered from that country, but which Russia had subsequently regained.

If Poland make such a claim as this, she is not very likely to establish it, and certainly, without passing any opinion on the question of her independence, one would naturally think that before she can enlist the sympathies of reflective people on her side, she will do well to waive such pretensions.

The Poles appear from their early history to have lived in plenty of hot water, and to have had their successes and reverses in about equal proportions. In 1772 took place the first partition of their country, which was planned and executed by Frederick II. of Prussia, notwithstanding that previously their old enemies, the Turks, had taken up arms in defence of Poland, after having vainly represented to some of the European cabinets the danger which might ensue were Russian influence and designs to become dominant in it.

By this partition Poland was deprived of some of its best provinces, which were taken possession of, though not in equal proportions, by Russia, Austria, and Prussia.

Shortly afterwards, an eminent Polish nobleman, Andrew Zamoyski, prepared a set of laws, removing many abuses, and to some extent emancipating the peasants.

These reforms were, however, objected to by the Polish Diet of 1780; and another Diet, which assembled in 1788, having declared itself permanent, continued till 1792, when it proclaimed a new constitution, declared the throne hereditary in the Saxon family (which was to take the crown after the death of the then reigning king, Poniatowski), and enacted some salutary laws of an enlightened nature. Russia and Prussia, however, took exception to these proceedings, and entered Poland with a large army, the result of which was that a second partition took place, by which, this time, Russia obtained the lion's share, and Poland was left with not more than about 85,000 square miles.

This residue of Poland was thereupon pretty well persecuted and harassed, and in the following year its people formed a plan for getting back the lost territory, and securing the independence of the kingdom. Kosciusko rushed to Cracow, and at the head of bands of peasants, armed chiefly with scythes, defeated and dispersed the Russian troops, who were greatly superior in numbers; but the fortunes of war, and, as usual, their own divided and jealous counsels, were against them; their enemies prevailed, and in 1795 what remained of Poland was divided between Russia and her two friends.

I never heard in Russia—for I was not in the way of hearing it—any arguments in favour of the Poles, and I don't know what may be the feeling in Poland with respect to the Russian Government, but, as a spectator, I must say that the manner in which the poorer class of people was treated by the Russian soldiery at some of the Polish places—Kowno, for instance—which we passed through, was brutal in the extreme. I don't attribute this conduct as a fault to the Russian Government, for it would be absurd to suppose, with the known kindly feelings of the Emperor, that he, as the head of it, would allow, or even countenance if he knew of it, such treatment of any of his subjects. The misconduct of the soldiery at Kowno, in driving, pushing, and beating the poor people away who came to the station simply to look about and indulge their very natural curiosity, was most reprehensible, and ought to have been checked by their superiors.

I can scarcely imagine that this state of things will continue for a very long time, and I suspect, if ever the Polish eagle should try another flight, that he will bite deep into his hereditary enemy.

No doubt the mind of the conquering is oftentimes bitter against the conquered race, and that whilst the former shows his teeth on every occasion, the latter covers them up, in the hope that "there is a good time coming."

I remember when in Milan, in 1857, walking down the main thoroughfare with an English gentleman. The Austrian officers, in the insolence of their power, used to walk down the street four or five abreast, and give no way, forcing all others into the road; and I remember, too, the fervent wishes we formed, and expressed pretty loudly, that their combs might soon be cut.

At that period we little thought in how few years the Austrians would be sent to the right-about, and have to make themselves scarce in Milan.

There was a circumstance which afterwards occurred to my friend and myself at Venice, which put us into a towering passion. We had arrived at Venice by the railroad, and were ushered into a great barn of a place to produce passports and have our baggage overhauled. It was in the middle of the month of March, and very cold. As all the doors were open, and no end of currents of wind playing rudely about us, we kept on our hats. Soon an official came up and ordered us to take them off. Of course we remonstrated against such a proceeding, saying that we should suffer in health by complying with his demand; and we pointed to several of the officials about the place whose heads were covered. To this our enemy rejoined that his orders were peremptory, and that as to the officials they were only wearing caps, not hats—the force of which distinction we did not clearly see.

However, the man pointed to a trumpery twopenny-halfpenny print of his Austrian Majesty hanging up in the room, and told us that it was to that we were to uncover, and that if we made any more demur we should be sent back to "the place whence we came." So, as there was no help for it, off went our hats, and a very nice cold I caught in consequence, which kept me some days a prisoner in the hotel.

I made the acquaintance at Creuznach, in the year following, of an Austrian colonel, to whom I one day mentioned this circumstance. He said that he could not believe such an occurrence could possibly have taken place at Venice, where the police had strict orders to be civil and obliging; but on tendering him the name and address of my friend, to whom he could write for confirmation, upon condition that he should stand a dinner for twelve if my friend confirmed the story, the colonel backed out, saying that the man at Venice had exceeded his authority.

I learned, a few days afterwards, that this colonel, who was really a very good sort of a fellow, and who used to amuse us by telling our fortunes from the lines in our hands, had been, or was, the head of the police at Venice. I heard, a year or two subsequently, that a great change had taken place in the conduct of the police authorities there, and many of my friends, to whom I related this "Gesler" story, assured me that they had met with a totally different treatment at that Venetian Douane.

Whether my friend the colonel had picked up better ideas in his travels, and put them into practice, I don't know, but he was just the sort of intelligent man who would put his experience to a practical issue.

Many Russians with whom I conversed on the subject of Poland, assimilated the position of the Poles towards Russia to the case of the Ionians towards England. I did not see the analogy, but I did see that there was evidently a jealous feeling against England continuing to hold the Ionian Islands.

What particular interest or views Russia may have in desiring those islands to be free from English protection, I do not profess to know. Earl Russell, our Foreign Secretary of State, may, perhaps, understand this matter, and see farther through a brick wall than the ordinary lot of mortals; but I confess that it did puzzle me to discover what motive actuated the Russian mind to go in for Ionian independence.

In due course we arrived at Pskoff, where we found the governor's carriage and servants waiting for us, and received a warm and hearty welcome at the hands of himself and his wife. Here we forgot all about passports and everything else that was unpleasant, until next morning, when the post arrived bringing no communication from our rascally courier. His Excellency, however, said he would make it all right for us, and the head of the police viséd our English Foreign-office passport, whilst the governor wrote something on one of the fly-leaves, and the seal of the province was duly affixed, to give it full weight and importance. "And," said his Excellency, pointing to what he had written, "if they make any demur at the frontier, show them that." So, after thanking him and his accomplished and ladylike wife for all their hospitality, and having, *more Russico*, received the governor's kiss on my cheek, we started at three o'clock P.M. for the railway, the chief of the police putting us into the railway carriage, and shaking hands most heartily with our friend at whose invitation we had gone to Russia, we went on our way to Berlin, which we hoped to reach in forty hours.

Alas! vain are the hopes of man, and woman too, in this vale of tears, especially in the Russian department of that vale where passports are in vogue. We passed through Kowno, congratulating ourselves that our destiny did not detain us there—short-sighted mortals that we are!—and arrived at the Russian frontier. Passports were demanded all round, and ours handed up, with a look at the official as much as to say, "Take your change out of that, young gentleman."

Here the train stops for an hour, and we walked about, and I pointed out the hole, still not filled up, into which I had nearly fallen in the dark, some weeks before, on our entrance into Russia. The sun was shining, all was quite serene, and we were in high spirits, when suddenly an officer in smart uniform, speaking English like a native of that foggy island, addressed me by my name, with my passport in his hand, blandly informing me, to my enormous disgust, that I could proceed no farther, as my passport was not *en règle.* "Ah!" thought I, "he has never looked at that fly-leaf." So with much self-importance I followed the Pskoff governor's admonition, and "showed him that." He politely laughed at my nose, as the French say, and told me that "that" was nothing—that it merely said the governor had no objection to my leaving Pskoff, but that he ought to have given me a Russian passport, as we had been more than seven days in the country, and he pointed to that tell-tale stamp which had been affixed to our English passport on our entering Russia. In vain were all representations. "You must go back to Kowno," said the official; that horrid place which we, four hours before, had congratulated ourselves on avoiding.

Before finally knocking under to the go-back-again decree, I bethought myself of that *fast* friend of the anxious, the telegraph. So I asked whether I should be allowed to pass the frontier in the event of my telegraphing to the governor at Pskoff, and obtaining his reply over the wires that my passport was all right, and received an answer in the affirmative.

Away I hurried to the bureau, and found a grey-coated militaire performing the duty which in England and France is discharged by a civilian.

This did not look very encouraging, but I explained my position and desire to send forward the telegram, which I was informed would be despatched immediately; but observing that he of the sword appeared to be either only half awake, or a novice at his work, I inquired how long it might probably take to get the governor's answer, when, to my surprise, I was told that if matters went smoothly, I might look for it between two and three o'clock in the morning of the following day.,

Now, seeing that Pskoff was in a direct line of telegraphic communication with the bureau, and that we had just done the distance by rail in about nineteen hours, it seemed very slow telegraphic work to require the same length of time to transmit a message and receive a reply.

But the grey-coated hero said it could

not be done under the time he had named, and appeared so surprised that any one should think otherwise, that I saw it was useless to make the attempt. So I left him alone in his glory, fagging away at the instruments upon which he had been engaged during the whole of our parley, and in the use of which I verily believe he was learning to perfect himself.

However, our last card was played and trumped, and all that we could then do was to smoke the cigar of resignation, and look cheerful.

In the absence of other amusement, our thoughts directed themselves to that breakfast of which we had heard on the road such appetising accounts, and which was always ready for the traveller when he reached the station on the Prussian frontier, but which, in our case, was too evidently postponed for twenty-four hours, if not for double that time.

We therefore set about making inquiries at the commissariat where we were, but all that we could find was some tea and stale pastry of a most unwholesome complexion, with any amount of spirits. So we walked off to breakfast on the sharp air, and speculate on the state of the larder at Kowno, a subsequent acquaintance with which did not very greatly prepossess us in its favour; but, as a Russian said to us afterwards, what could you expect in a dirty little Polish town?

Away went the train to Berlin, and we "were left lamenting." Soon after, a young German gentleman, who had heard the whole proceeding, told us that if we chose to employ and pay one of the Jews living near he would get us across the frontier in time for the afternoon train. This course, however, we declined, and the circumstance is only mentioned to show that, generally speaking, the passport system may be simply an inconvenience to the scrupulous, but no check upon the unscrupulous person. I learned afterwards that numbers evade the passport regulations by these means.

The train came up from Prussia two hours afterwards, and we went back to Kowno, four hours from the frontier. It was raining and blowing hard, and we were awfully disgusted with our position, for now we had no courier, and I did not clearly see my way to making myself understood in that Polish village. However, a tidy little man fastened upon us the moment we put foot in the station-house. He told us that of course we were going to the Hôtel de France, and, as he spoke German, we thought we might do worse; so, after a drive of a mile, with the water up to the axletrees, we found ourselves safely housed. The landlord was a German, and to him "we did unload our grief." He seemed to be quite accustomed to that sort of event, and told us we had only to give our English passport to our little friend, and that all would be arranged before the evening. And so it was; and before tea-time we had a great long document in the Russian language safe in our possession, and next morning, at half-past four, were under way again for the train that was to take us once more to the frontier. If any of our fellow-countrymen find themselves in a similar predicament, I recommend them to do as we did, but to keep a rather sharp look-out that the tidy little man does not do them out of too many of their roubles: he did us to the tune of about a hundred per cent., which I did not find out till afterwards. He, however, kissed our hands at parting, laughing, no doubt, at the successful way in which he had done Mr. and Mrs. Bull.

We did not see much of Kowno. It stands at the confluence of the Wilia and the Niemen, has about eight thousand inhabitants, and does a good trade. Some of the streets were pretty fair, but on the whole I should say there is little inducement to a tourist to stop there. It was not far from here that Napoleon crossed the Niemen in June, 1812, on his way to Moscow, and it was near here also that the remnant of his grand army crossed in the December following. Again we arrived at the frontier, and again we found our bland friend in uniform. Our passport was declared all right, but not so that of a very stylish and good-looking woman of about thirty-five years old.

We naturally watched the proceeding with some interest, and I was just about to recommend to her my friend at Kowno, when, after a little more parleying, the lady resumed her seat, and we soon saw her within the Prussian frontier as busy as a bee, looking after her baggage and breakfast. "An unprotected female" is always more or less an object of interest, and so we did not feel angry that the favour that had been granted in her case had been refused in ours. With this little incident terminated our visit to Russia, and in twenty-eight hours after leaving her frontier we arrived in the quiet old city of Hanover, bringing away with us innumerable recollections of the kindness and hospitality we had received from our Russian friends and acquaintances.

I have spoken in previous chapters of the intemperance of the Russian peasant, but it is only just towards him that the whole truth should be known. Talking to a Russian gentleman during our enforced journey to Kowno, and alluding to this subject as a matter to be much deplored, he took the peasant's part, and showed how bad was the system of the excise-laws with regard to the sale of spirituous liquors, and what evil results followed in its wake.

It appeared from his statement that for a long period it has been the custom of the Russian Government to put up to auction the right of farming the sale of spirits.

This right is sold to one person or set of persons for each province, and for the whole of Russia the sale produced no less than one hundred and twenty millions of roubles, or four millions eight hundred thousand pounds English, for each of the years 1860, '61, and '62—a sum constituting about two-fifths of the whole annual revenue of the empire.

In the centre of Russia, and in all the towns and cities, the farmers alone had the right of selling spirits wholesale or retail. The spirits were sold by the distillers to the Government at a price fixed by itself, and the Government sold them to the farmers, who had also the power of imposing an arbitrary tax, payable in advance, upon cellars, restaurants, cafés, and all houses where spirits were sold.

The farmer, in return, was bound to sell at a price fixed by the Government; but this obligation was never observed, and he sold at any sum he chose to name, and, in addition, adulterated the article to a pretty considerable extent. The consequence of which was that he amassed a large fortune.

To conceal his rascality, and to save himself from being hauled over the coals, the farmer was obliged to bribe the local authorities, from the highest down to the lowest, so that the farmer of a province often paid away in bribes as much as 2000*l.* a year.

By means such as these the local police and authorities in many districts were entirely under his control, and, as a matter of course, he cheated away right and left, sold all sorts of adulterated abominations, and feathered his nest with the plunder.

In 1858, the peasants, seeing how they were cheated, and unable to get any protection from the bribed guardians of the law, set to work and established temperance, or rather, I should say, total abstinence, societies.

The members of these societies swore to observe a total abstinence from the use of all spirituous liquors, and went to their village churches, asking the priests to say a *Te Deum* in order to obtain from the Almighty strength enough to observe their oaths.

A striking proof, by the way, that the Russian serf is endued with the first and best principles of that intelligence which points the way to freedom and civilisation.

In a country like Russia, with its alternating degrees of heat and cold, amongst a population exposed at all times and seasons to the vicissitudes of the weather, no foreigner can well judge of the privations to which the peasants were voluntarily subjecting themselves by joining such societies as these.

Rightly or wrongly, they imagined that spirituous liquors were a necessity. They who argue that men, whether living in the fens of Holland or in the wilds of Russia, require no stimulating drinks, may be right, for aught I know; but the Russian peasant has no such belief; he thinks that spirits are as necessary to him as the air he breathes, and, therefore, the privation to which he voluntarily doomed himself deserves the favourable construction which unprejudiced minds would accord to him.

But mark the sequel. The farmers took alarm. What! not drink? they said. Not buy our adulterations?

So they applied to the Government, and completely frightened it. They could not, they said, pay the amounts they had agreed to pay, and the revenue of the Government must suffer, unless strong measures were immediately adopted. In a word, if the people who had desired to drink good and cheap drinks were not enforced to drink the farmers' abominations, the safety and welfare of the nation were gone, with the revenue on which the nation depended.

The farmers then obtained from the ministers of the Crown a decree that no association for any purpose whatever was legal, or could be permitted to exist, unless the consent of the Crown in its favour had been previously obtained. It was easy enough to show that that consent had never been granted in favour of temperance societies. Therefore temperance societies were declared illegal, and their members were put under the ban.

In a mode peculiarly Russian, the police, the bribed friends of the spirit farmers, went about in the country districts, and at the end of the stick compelled the peasants to buy and drink, until in some places, roused to fury, the peasants rose and burnt the drinking-houses.

But in the same year, 1858, when the farming was for the last time put up to auction, the present Emperor Alexander expressed his sorrow at seeing so large a part of the country's revenue derived from so disgraceful a source, and, as usual in any great abuse, he took the necessary steps to remove it.

The whole question was by his orders submitted to a council of the empire, and they advised his Majesty to abolish the old system and initiate a new one, founded upon the principles and practice adopted in England.

The result is, that, on the 31st of December, 1862, the regulations for distilling and selling spirituous liquors, and of licensing houses for the sale of them, is made to correspond with the regulations in force in England, and the day of the farmers has seen its night.

And so in effect the peasants conquered! But they conquered solely through the firmness of the Emperor against that powerful retrograde party in the empire, who, looking only to their own gains and profits, would hold the whole people of Russia in a servile and disgraceful subjection to secure their own selfish ends.

In England it is somewhat the fashion to withhold praise from the Emperor of Russia. My own opinion, founded on what I heard, is that, although the system of government there is not one under which I should care to live, the Emperor himself is a kind, well-intentioned man, and would do even more good than he actually performs, were he not restrained by some of his own subjects.

I was told that his Majesty contemplates, and was even then devising, a plan for a constitutional government more in accordance with the feelings, ideas, and opinions of the country from which he had taken his system of excise laws with respect to the sale of spirituous liquors.

Whether his people are sufficiently ripe for that sort of thing (I allude to the higher, not the humbler, classes) is more than I can tell. I should fear that the majority are not to be trusted with any great amount of power at present, but I hope that the day cannot be far distant when the enlightened principles which now distinguish the minority will be acknowledged by, and govern the actions of, the educated classes of the great Russian empire.

THE END.